Renée jumped inside her skin at the deep, throaty rumble.

Tall, broad-shouldered, wearing a sheepskin jacket and a cowboy hat, the stranger joined them. Her gaze traveled the length of his long jean-clad legs, stopping at his snakeskin boots.

The cowboy grinned. "Duke Dalton."

Duke? What kind of a name was that?

His large hand swallowed hers, and she held on longer than necessary, soaking up the heat from his calloused fingers. "Why don't we discuss this over dinner?"

There were worse things than sharing a meal with a citified cowboy. A gut feeling insisted that beneath the cowboy persona, the man meant her no harm. But she feared she'd need a miracle to persuade him to hold off on his plans for the building.

'Tis the season for miracles.

Who knew? Maybe Duke Dalton would turn out to be *her* Christmas miracle.

Dear Reader,

When one thinks of Detroit, Michigan, they think cars. Motown. Sports. They also think poverty, economic depression and crime. If one looks beyond the troubled car industry and foreclosing homes, the Motor City is a community of rhythm and passion. You will discover in this book that Detroiters of all ages are strong, resilient survivors—there's no better backdrop for a Christmas story.

I've teamed up an unlikely pair—a corporate CEO, Duke Dalton, and a Detroit social worker, Renée Sweeney. Together they must figure out how to pull off a Christmas miracle for those who deserve it most—children. And in the process Duke and Renée will discover their very own happily-ever-after.

This season may the holiday spirit fill your heart with the joy of giving. Let us not forget the children in our communities who are waiting to experience the miracle of Christmas.

For information on my upcoming books, please visit www.marinthomas.com or contact me at marin@marinthomas.com.

Happy Holidays!

Marin

The Cowboy and the Angel
MARIN THOMAS

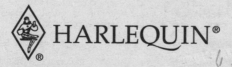

HARLEQUIN®

TORONTO • NEW YORK • LONDON
AMSTERDAM • PARIS • SYDNEY • HAMBURG
STOCKHOLM • ATHENS • TOKYO • MILAN • MADRID
PRAGUE • WARSAW • BUDAPEST • AUCKLAND

ISBN-13: 978-0-373-75240-9
ISBN-10:   0-373-75240-7

THE COWBOY AND THE ANGEL

www.eHarlequin.com

Printed in U.S.A.

ABOUT THE AUTHOR

Typical of small-town kids, all Marin Thomas, born in Janesville, Wisconsin, could think about was how to leave after she graduated from high school.

Her six-foot-one-inch height was her ticket out. She accepted a basketball scholarship at the University of Missouri in Columbia, where she studied journalism. After two years she transferred to University of Arizona at Tucson, where she played center for the Lady Wildcats. While at Arizona, she developed an interest in fiction writing and obtained a B.A. in radio-television. Marin was inducted in May 2005 into the Janesville Sports Hall of Fame for her basketball accomplishments.

Her husband's career in public relations has taken them to Arizona, California, New Jersey, Colorado, Texas and Illinois, where she currently calls Chicago her home. Marin can now boast that she's seen what's "out there." Amazingly enough, she's a living testament to the old adage "You can take the girl out of the small town, but you can't take the small town out of the girl." Her heart still lies in small-town life, which she loves to write about in her books.

Books by Marin Thomas

HARLEQUIN AMERICAN ROMANCE

1024—THE COWBOY AND THE BRIDE
1050—DADDY BY CHOICE
1079—HOMEWARD BOUND
1124—AARON UNDER CONSTRUCTION*
1148—NELSON IN COMMAND*
1165—SUMMER LOVIN'
        "The Preacher's Daughter"
1175—RYAN'S RENOVATION *
1184—FOR THE CHILDREN **
1200—IN A SOLDIER'S ARMS**
1224—A COAL MINER'S WIFE**

*The McKade Brothers
**Hearts of Appalachia

To my former college basketball teammates from the University of Arizona in Tucson: Kirsten Smith-Cambron, Yolanda Turner, Alicia Archie, Angie Dodds-Seymour and Dana Patterson. What a privilege it was to run the court with you ladies. Thanks for the memories!

Go Wildcats!!

Chapter One

Renée Sweeney stood defiantly in front of the ten-ton wrecking ball and glared at the crane operator inside the cab. The man's mouth twisted from side to side, but she couldn't hear a word over the rumbling engine— probably a good thing. No doubt he was spewing cuss words.

Too bad. If she had her way the 1892 Screw & Bolt Factory Warehouse along the historical Detroit River-front would stay standing—long enough for her to come up with a plan for the six little problems taking refuge inside the marked building.

The brisk December wind shoved her off balance, but she locked her knees and managed to remain upright. A moment later, the squeal of the machine's grinding gears ceased and an eerie silence reverberated through the air. *Thank goodness.*

The operator climbed from the cab and jabbed a meaty finger in her direction. "Hey, lady! What the hell are you doing?"

Wasn't it obvious? She stared at the man without answering.

"I'm calling the cops," he raged, pulling a cell phone from his coat pocket, then trudged out of hearing range.

If his wild arm gestures were any indication, the 911 operator was receiving an earful.

Renée snuggled deeper into her white ankle-length goose-down coat. In her rush to reach the Riverfront, she'd grabbed her scarf but had forgotten her gloves. The day's high of thirty-eight was losing ground fast against the projected overnight low of ten degrees. She hoped she'd accomplish her mission before all ten of her digits blackened from frostbite. At least the scarf prevented her ears from curling up and dropping off her head.

With watery eyes she searched for a windbreak, but the few barren trees that called the concrete parking lot home were useless. She was tempted to take shelter in the giant holly bushes that hid the first floor of the building, but feared the crane operator would set the ball swinging at her retreat. Once in a while her job as a social worker required creative action to protect children at risk, but challenging a wrecking ball was a bit extreme and Renée doubted her boss would approve.

Across the parking lot a handful of construction workers huddled inside their vehicles, smoking cigarettes while their boss dealt with this latest interruption. A hot coffee from the men would have been a nice thank-you for shortening the end of their workweek.

Her stomach grumbled, reminding her that she'd skipped lunch. She glanced at her watch. Four o'clock. In a few minutes the cops would arrive. Hopefully by the time the police sent her on her way with a warning, it would be too dark to proceed with the demolition.

The crane operator snapped his cell phone shut, tossed a furious look over his shoulder, then proceeded to make another call—probably the fire department in the event Detroit's finest were engaged in more important activities such as apprehending real criminals. She wiped her runny nose on the back of her coat sleeve and stared at the river across the street. This time of year few boats navigated the chunks of ice floating on the water, turning the Riverfront into a nautical ghost town. The Screw & Bolt building sat in the middle of the warehouse district among several turn-of-the-century structures.

The area was desolate, and she questioned the sanity of the fool who'd purchased the derelict property between the Renaissance Center and Belle Isle. A short while ago she'd chatted with her brother, a Detroit police officer, and he'd mentioned seeing the demolition equipment as he'd patrolled the area. In a panic, she'd rushed to the warehouse, praying she'd arrive before disaster struck.

Rocking forward on the balls of her feet, she added another inch to her five-foot-five height and braced herself for round two as the crane operator marched toward her, the stub of an unlit cigar bobbing between his fleshy blue lips. Eyes narrowed, he paused several feet away. His yellow hard hat left his ears exposed and they glowed the same bright red color as the bulbous tip of his nose.

"I don't know what your cause is, lady. Don't much give a shit. I've been paid to demolish this building and haul the rubble away by the end of next week. If I miss that deadline, I lose a lotta money." He motioned to the group of idling trucks. "You wouldn't want those guys going without pay, seeing how their kids are expecting gifts from Santa under the tree in a few weeks."

Renée had a soft spot for children—why else would she do a fool thing like take on a construction crane in the bitter cold? If the workers went without a paycheck, their kids might not receive every item on their Santa wish list, but at least they'd have a roof over their heads and a warm meal on Christmas day—which was more than she could say for the kids she hoped to protect from Bob the Builder and his demolition crew.

Police sirens whined through the air, saving her the trouble of responding. A squad car screeched to a stop and two officers stepped from the vehicle. *Drat!* Her brother, Rich, and his partner, Pete, had taken the call.

"Hi, guys," Renée said when the cops drew within hearing distance. She wanted to offer her brother a reassuring smile, but feared her bottom lip would split open and drip blood onto her white coat.

Pete's gaze swung from the crane to the construction foreman to Renée. Rich leveled a what-have-you-gone-and-done-now glare at her, then stood sentry at her side. A silent laugh shook her chest when the cigar tumbled from the foreman's mouth and bounced off the top of his steel-toe work boot.

Over the years, she'd developed friendships with several Detroit policemen. Often she required their assistance in removing children from abusive homes and placing them into protective custody. The officers understood and turned a blind eye when Renée bent the rules to do what was best for the child. She prayed her brother and his partner would cut her some slack this afternoon.

As dusk shrouded the parking lot like a heavy cloak, concealing the water, piers and moorings along the river, a chorus of revving truck engines erupted and the work crew left.

"What's going on?" Pete asked.

Grabbing at straws, she said, "I'm not sure this gentleman has obtained the proper permit to demolish this building."

Rich gaped at her as if she'd lost her mind.

Pete came to her rescue. "Mind if I see the paperwork?"

The foreman stomped his boot like a two-year-old throwing a temper tantrum and demanded, "Who the hell is this woman?"

"Watch your mouth, mister," Rich warned.

Sputtering, her adversary returned to the crane, crawled inside the cab, flung things around, then stormed back across the pavement. Hot air spewed out of his nostrils, forming a misty cloud above his head. "Work orders." He shoved the papers at Pete.

A twinge of empathy for the irate man caught Renée by surprise, but she pushed it aside. She needed the warehouse more than the foreman needed to swing his wrecking ball.

"Appears official," Pete said.

"Then she's gotta haul ass and get out of the way, right?" A fleck of spittle at the corner of his mouth froze into a white ice ball.

"Depends…"

"On what?" The man's gaze dropped to Pete's gun holster.

"Whether the permit is on file at city hall."

"How the heck should I know? That's the property owner's responsibility. My job is to demolish this hell-hole."

"Tomorrow's Saturday," Rich cut in. "City hall is closed. We'll verify the permit first thing Monday morning. Until then you'll have to shut down."

"What seems to be the problem here, Mr. Santori?"

Renée jumped inside her skin at the deep, throaty rumble and spun. Tall, broad shouldered, wearing a sheepskin jacket and a cowboy hat—a ridiculous choice of headgear for freezing weather—the stranger joined the group. Her gaze traveled the length of his long jean-clad legs, stopping at his snakeskin boots. He was no ordinary cowboy who'd wandered in off the range. This roper reeked of money. Renée immediately disliked him.

"Mr. Dalton, this broad—"

Rich cleared his throat nosily, and Mr. Santori amended, "—this *lady* planted herself in front of the crane and refused to budge. What was I supposed to do? Bean her in the head with twenty-thousand pounds of steel?"

The cowboy grinned and Renée wished she had an object to *bean* him with. "No, we certainly don't want any harm to come to...?" His sexy voice trailed off and a few seconds passed before she collected her scattered wits.

"Renée Sweeney."

"Duke Dalton."

Duke? What kind of name was that? Sounded like a moniker one would give a bulldog or porn star.

Mr. Dalton's large, bare grip swallowed hers, and she held on longer than necessary, soaking up the heat from his calloused fingers. After he shook hands with Pete and Rich, a tense silence followed.

Disgusted, Mr. Santori nodded at her. "This one's all yours, Mr. Dalton. Unless I hear otherwise, I'll be back with my crew bright and early Monday morning." Muttering under his breath, the grumpy man headed for his truck.

Renée turned to Mr. Dalton. "You are aware this is Detroit?" The hair peeking out from under his cowboy hat was a rich brown color with a few auburn strands thrown in for contrast. "Texas is west of the Mississippi."

Pete and Rich chuckled.

Stone-faced, the cowboy ignored her sass. "What organization are you representing?"

Organization? "I'm not. This building—" she pointed behind her "—has historical value and shouldn't be touched." In truth several of the warehouses along the river had historical significance, but that didn't guarantee they'd stand in place forever.

"There's not much left of the building worth saving," Mr. Dalton said. "I investigated the possibility of restoring the structure, but the cost was prohibitive. Cheaper to build new."

Surprised the man had done his homework, Renée struggled to respond. She suspected the bitter temps had caused the neurons in her brain to misfire, impeding her ability to speak. Pete nudged her shoulder. Neither cop would depart until she did. Time to end the standoff. But how? A blast of wind seared her chaffed face and caused her teeth to clatter.

"Why don't we discuss this over dinner," Mr. Dalton suggested.

There were worse things than sharing a meal with a citified cowboy—like becoming a human Popsicle. "The Railway Diner is a few blocks over. Let's meet there."

Ignoring her brother's we'll-talk-later look, she shuffled on numb feet to her car. Once inside the wagon, she cranked the engine and blasted the heat, which made her nose drip like a faucet. While Rich detained Mr. Dalton—no doubt to impart a warning to behave himself around her—she pressed her hands against the air vents until her knuckles thawed enough that she was able to bend her fingers and grasp the steering wheel.

Although she appreciated her brother's concern, she trusted her instincts. Reading between the lines and deciphering truth from lies was a necessary skill in her line of work. A gut feeling insisted that beneath the cowboy persona, the man meant her no ill will or harm.

He may be decent, but he's not a pushover.

Renée feared she'd need a miracle to persuade him to hold off on his plans for the building.

'Tis the season for miracles.

Maybe Duke Dalton would turn out to be Renée's Christmas miracle.

DUKE WATCHED Renée Sweeney drive off in her 2005 silver Ford Focus station wagon—not the kind of vehicle he'd have expected a woman with a feisty personality to drive. He pictured the spitfire in a red Mustang.

When Santori had phoned about a disturbance at the work site, Duke had expected to find a group of protesters chained to the building door, not a pint-size woman going toe-to-toe with a wrecking ball.

"She's one of our city's most popular social workers," the cop named Pete boasted.

The blonde was a social worker? She'd looked more like an avenging angel in her long white coat and matching scarf. The woman intrigued Duke and he was eager to learn her reasons for delaying the demolition of his building.

"Renée's special." The gleam in the other officer's eyes told Duke to mind his manners. The cop had to be in his fifties and the social worker hadn't appeared to be a day over thirty. Were they a couple? Duke hadn't made friends since moving to Detroit a month ago. He would have enjoyed becoming better acquainted with Ms. Sweeney, but he refused to trespass on another man's territory.

"You mess with Renée, you mess with us. Got it?" the old guy threatened.

"Understood." Duke hustled across the lot, eager to escape the cold. The below-freezing temps that had blanketed the state the past week had him second-guessing his decision to move his business from Tulsa to Detroit. He'd take an occasional paralyzing ice storm any day over the below-zero temperatures of this Midwest meat locker.

Once inside his truck, he revved the engine and flipped on the heat. Even though the policeman had made it clear that Renée Sweeney was off-limits, anticipation stirred Duke's gut. Having eaten alone since arriving in the Motor City, he was ready to engage in conversation with someone other than himself. And he expected the social worker had plenty to say. He'd caught the way she'd summed him up with a cold, hard stare and he anticipated changing her uncomplimentary opinion of him.

When Duke pulled into the parking lot of the Railway Diner he recalled his Realtor suggesting the burger joint months ago when he'd been in town signing the closing papers on the warehouse property. He parked three spaces away from the silver wagon. Leaving his hat in the truck, he hurried toward the entrance where Renée stood inside the door.

"How long for a table?" He leaned closer to hear her response in the crowded waiting area and detected a hint of perfume in her hair—a nice change from the smell of fishy river water and wet decay that saturated the air along the Riverfront.

"Five minutes or less."

He slipped out of his coat, then offered to help Renée with hers, but she scooted aside and shed her own jacket. If she was averse to his touch, why had she shaken his hand in the parking lot? Better yet—why had her fingers clung to his so long?

The hostess rescued them from further awkward conversation, and they ascended the steps to the dining area. Halfway through the car, grilled onions and frying beef assaulted his nose. He'd have to send his clothes off to be laundered tonight if he hoped to prevent his hotel room from smelling like fried hamburger.

Duke waited for Renée to scoot into the booth, then he sat across from her. A waitress named Peggy arrived with menus and water glasses. "Half-price burgers on Fridays," she announced. "Coffee?"

"Please." Renée's smile knocked the wind from Duke. The woman had dimples in both cheeks and beautiful, straight white teeth.

Peggy cleared her throat and his neck warmed at having been caught gawking. "Make that two coffees." When the waitress disappeared, he said, "Smile."

Renée raised an eyebrow. "Why?"

"I want to see your dimples again."

She rolled her eyes, then complied—not a sweet smile, but a bite-you-in-the-ass smirk. Darned if those tiny pits in the middle of her cheeks weren't the sexiest, most impudent dents he'd seen in a long time. His gaze traveled from her cheeks to her mouth, then to her electric-blue eyes. Renée Sweeney was a very pretty woman.

And he'd been warned away from her.

The mental prompt didn't stop him from ogling as she perused the menu. Her bulky coat had disguised her figure, but her pink cable-knit sweater flaunted her femininity, clinging to the gentle swells of her breasts. Dainty fingers sported neatly trimmed nails painted in a frosted-pink color to match the sweater. Every inch of the woman shouted *cuddle me.* Too bad the cop had already claimed snuggling rights.

"You're staring."

"Sorry. I'm in awe—" *of your beauty* "—that such a small woman took on an entire construction crew."

"I won, didn't I?" she boasted.

Laughter boomed from his chest. "Yes, you did." Beauty and pride—a winning combination in his book. Too bad she didn't act the least bit interested in him.

Waitress Peggy delivered their coffee, then flipped open her order pad.

"I'll have seven plain cheeseburgers and seven servings of fries," Renée said.

The pencil tip broke against the pad. "I'm sorry. How many burgers did you say?"

"Seven burgers. Seven fries. And six of those orders will be to-go."

"Okaaay. Sir?"

"One burger. One fry." He handed Peggy his menu. As soon as she left, he teased, "All that fresh air gave you an appetite."

"Hardly." Then she not-so-subtly changed the subject. "You aren't a Michigan native."

"I was born in St. Louis. My mother and I moved to Oklahoma when I was thirteen years old." Under protest from Duke. He'd hoped his workaholic mother would make more time for him after his father had died, but he'd been sadly mistaken. Within a year of his father's death, his mother had accepted Dominick Cartwright's marriage proposal and suddenly Duke had had to share his mother with two stepsiblings.

"Thought I detected a twang." Renée smiled.

He grimaced. He prided himself on having dropped his Okie accent when he'd attended college at UCLA.

"What are your plans for the warehouse property?" she asked, ending polite conversation.

"I'm relocating my company, Dalton Industries, from Tulsa to Detroit. I intend to flatten the warehouse and erect a new building, which will house company offices and condos."

"What does Dalton Industries do?"

Was she genuinely interested in his company or working up to some…*point* she intended to make? If he wasn't careful he'd forget Ms. Sweeney's agenda interfered with his. Still, it had been a long time since he'd had the opportunity to share his dream with anyone other than business partners, Realtors, construction crews and architects. "Dalton Industries is a player in the information and technology arena." When she stared at him expectantly, he continued, "My company will lead the way in the city's efforts to revitalize the warehouse district along the Detroit River."

She snorted.

Startled, he demanded, "What?"

"Nothing." She shifted her attention from his face to the napkin holder at the end of the table.

"Tell me."

Her dainty chin lifted and her facial muscles pulled into a pinched glare. "The wealthy businessmen I've had run-ins with in the past convinced me that their goals rank higher in importance than doing the right thing."

What gave her the impression Duke was wealthy? "The fact that I own a business doesn't mean I'm drowning in money." To tell the truth one of the reasons he'd moved his company had been to escape the influence of his stepfather. Dominick's offer to invest in Dalton Industries had been heartfelt, but Duke needed to prove he could stand on his own two feet without the aid of Cartwright oil money. Like hundreds of other businessmen, he'd taken out bank loans to finance his venture.

A pink-tipped finger flicked at his head. "Your haircut alone probably cost a hundred bucks."

He ran a hand through his hair, leaving several previously immaculate layers mussed. "Thirty-five dollars and that included a five-dollar tip."

She frowned. "Snakeskin boots?"

"A gift from my mother." The last birthday present he'd received from her before she died in a car accident two years ago.

"Your name."

"What's wrong with Duke?"

"Sounds stuck-up. Like royalty."

"I was named after my maternal grandfather, Duke Weatherford. He was a science professor at Cambridge University." Duke didn't appreciate being deemed unacceptable because of his name, but damned if he'd defend himself.

Then she slapped him with another stinging question. "Why bring your company to Detroit when it's obvious you don't fit in here?"

Maybe he stood out now, but with time he intended to become a true Detroiter. And Michigan was the farthest thing from ranches, oil and his stepfather's influence—he doubted anyone this far north had heard of the multimillionaire. "The city made an offer I couldn't refuse."

Her eyes narrowed. "You mean steep tax breaks."

"Yes, tax breaks. But my company will contribute to the general revitalization fund to improve the Riverfront." What he didn't confess was that Detroit was the only city whose financial incentives enabled him to transfer his company without having to accept a handout from his stepfather. His turn to change the subject. "Your boyfriend informed me that you were a social worker."

"Boyfriend?"

"The older cop seemed pretty possessive of you."

"Rich? He's not my boyfriend. He's my brother."

Siblings? They looked nothing alike. Renée had beautiful blond hair and the cop was a carrottop. Relief pulsed through Duke's body, and he grinned like a fool.

He had no qualms about ignoring an older brother's warning. If Duke had his way, tonight's dinner would be the beginning of his getting-to-know-Ms.-Renée-Sweeney-better campaign. But just in case... "Any other boyfriends or big brothers in the picture?"

"No, I'm unattached at the moment."

Unattached was good. Very good.

"The Screw & Bolt factory has been a part of the Riverfront for a long, long time," she argued, showing no interest in pursuing a personal conversation with him.

"I'm aware of the building's significance. I read up on the area before I put in an offer."

Her soft huff claimed she didn't believe him. Time for a history lesson. "The factory was established in 1877 on Lafayette before moving to Atwater and Riopelle in 1892." He paused, expecting an apology—nothing. "The company erected a new building in 1912. They manufactured cap screws, nuts and automobile parts, then went out of business before World War II. From then on the building was used as a warehouse for various companies until it became permanently vacant."

"Okay, you did your homework," she conceded. Peggy arrived with the burgers and a large to-go bag. Renée thanked her, then proceeded to devour her meal.

Why the rush? He'd hoped to discover if they shared a common interest besides an old warehouse. "How long have you been a social worker?"

"Six years."

"Born and raised in Detroit?"

A single nod. "What does a social worker want with an abandoned building?" he prodded.

With great care, she set her burger on the plate and finished chewing. "What if I asked you to hold off destroying the warehouse for a month?"

Nice try. "You didn't answer my question."

A stare-down ensued. He gave in first. "No." He didn't dare delay construction. The lease on the current office building in Tulsa expired in September of next year, leaving nine months to complete his new headquarters. In truth, there wasn't enough money in the coffers to pay additional rent in Oklahoma.

"A few weeks won't make a difference," Renée argued. "Besides, it's freezing outside. No one pours cement in the middle of winter."

Unwilling to be swayed, he remained silent. Her eyes flashed with irritation, their blue color brightening. Then she blurted, "Give me one week."

Obviously she had no intention of coming clean with him. Duke didn't want any part of whatever scheme this woman was involved in. For all he knew, she might be breaking the law. Dinner had been a disappointing waste of time. Too bad they hadn't met under different circumstances. Renée was the first woman he'd encountered in Detroit who intrigued him and he balked at the idea of never seeing her again. Blaming indigestion for the churning feeling in his gut, he slid from the booth, leaving his half-eaten burger on the plate. "I can't agree to a day, much less a week."

Renée's mouth sagged. "You're going to leave before we've finished discussing the subject?"

He wouldn't label their conversation a discussion—more like a one-sided argument. He removed a fifty-dollar bill from his wallet and tossed it on the table, then grabbed his coat. "As far as I'm concerned there's nothing more to say." Hoping she'd change her mind, he paused with one arm shoved inside his coat sleeve. Her mutinous glare vowed she wasn't budging from her position. He fished a pen and a business card from his pocket, then scrawled the name of his hotel and room number on the back.

"What's this?" She held the card between her fingertips as if it was contaminated with germs.

"For whenever you're ready to confess the truth. Unless I learn what you're really after, Renée, the wrecking ball swings on Monday."

Chapter Two

A *click-click-clicking* sound greeted Renée when she let herself in the door of her mother's two-bedroom cottage on Church Street in Corktown—Detroit's oldest neighborhood. "Hey, Mom, it's me!"

"In here, honey."

Renée stowed the half-gallon of ice cream she'd brought over in the freezer, then dropped her purse on the gold-flecked Formica countertop in the kitchen. After ditching her coat, she joined her mother in the living room. As expected, seventy-nine-year-old Bernice sat in the recliner watching *COPS* on TV, her knobby, arthritic fingers moving a pair of knitting needles at lightning speed. Row after row of gray yarn piled high in her lap. The almost-empty wicker basket next to the chair served as a reminder that Renée needed to take her mother yarn shopping.

Bernice Sweeney knitted afghans and sweaters, which she donated to city shelters and the neighborhood Most Holy Trinity Church's winter clothing drive.

Expelling an exasperated breath Renée dropped onto the couch. She hadn't been able to purge Duke Dalton from her mind since their dinner date—correction, dinner *meeting*—Friday. The quick meal with the cowboy had been the closest to a date she'd come in months.

Peering over the rim of her bifocals Bernice asked, "Anything wrong?"

"No." *Yes*. Why did the new owner of the Screw & Bolt Factory have to be handsome? Mannerly? As stubborn as she was? Renée offered a smile, not wishing to worry her mother—a woman who'd spent her entire adult life glancing at clocks and waiting for the phone to ring with bad news.

Gun shots exploded from the TV and for a moment Renée watched the drama unfold. She'd stopped second-guessing her mother's addiction to *COPS* long ago, figuring the series provided a therapeutic purpose. Bernice's husband had been a Detroit cop killed in the line of duty thirty-one years ago. Renée was sad that Bernice had lost her husband at a young age and in such a violent manner, but if not for the tragedy Bernice would never have adopted Renée. And she couldn't imagine her life without Bernice and Rich in it.

As soon as the suspect on TV had been apprehended, Renée's mother spoke. "Something's bothering you."

Not something…*someone*. "I'm fine," Renée fudged. While running her usual Saturday errands she'd agonized over Duke Dalton's warning. She feared the man hadn't been bluffing when he'd threatened to destroy the warehouse Monday.

The *clickity-clack* stopped and a thick gray eyebrow arched. "You were just over here last night."

Renée's home sat next door to her mother's. She'd purchased the two-bedroom, one bathroom cottage three years ago. With the help of her brother she'd scraped together enough cash for the down payment. "Can't a daughter spend time with her mother?" It ticked off Renée that her encounter with Duke had unnerved her to the point where she acted like a wimpy kid in need of mommy's hug.

Darn the cowboy. Not only did he worry her…he excited her. When she'd sat across from him in the booth the previous night, every pore in her body had opened wide and absorbed his appearance, his smell, his voice…his sophistication. But it was his gentle brown eyes that caused her the most grief. They begged her to trust him.

A bad, bad idea.

"Go be bored in your own house." Although a loving smile accompanied the command, Renée believed Bernice used her stubborn independence as a shield against the fear of becoming a burden to her children. "No hot date tonight?" her mother teased.

"I'm thirty-one. Hot dates are for hormonal teenagers." Duke's face flashed through her mind and she decided he could easily make her hormonal if he cared to.

"I brought ice cream." Renée sprang from the couch and gave her mother an impulsive hug, breathing in the almond scent of Jergens lotion before skipping off to the kitchen.

Out of sight, she slumped over the counter and rubbed her fingers against her forehead in rhythmic circles. She hadn't been able to shake the headache that had chiseled away at her frontal lobe all afternoon. After shoveling Rocky Road into two bowls, she and her mother enjoyed their treat in silence. Bernice finished first. "If you don't tell me what's bothering you, I can't fix it."

How Renée wished her mother had the power to mend the predicament Renée had gotten herself into. She changed the subject. "Have you agreed to go out to dinner with Mr. Morelli yet?" Mr. Morelli was the self-appointed block warden. The old coot marched along Church Street leaving notes on the front doors of homes in violation of the neighborhood beautification program.

"Roberto's too young for me," Bernice sputtered.

"There's only five years difference between the two of you." After seventy did age matter?

"He has bad breath."

"Tell him to try a different denture cream."

Her mother rolled her eyes. "What makes you an expert on men, young lady?"

Touché. Bernice made no bones about the fact that before she strolled up to the pearly gates, she wanted her daughter married with children. With Renée's nonexistent dating life, the likelihood of fulfilling her mother's wish was equally nonexistent.

"What about that nice young man Rich introduced you to a month ago?"

Disaster. Renée had warned Rich that she didn't care to date cops. She loved her brother and supported his choice of careers, but marry a police officer? *No way.* She fretted enough over the children under her care. She didn't need the added angst of worrying that her husband might not live through his next shift. "Ben and I didn't click." No sense stating the particulars—like Ben had a potty mouth and a habit of denigrating the women who worked the street corners in Detroit's less reputable neighborhoods. Or that Ben had been married before—twice. Renée wasn't interested in becoming strike number three.

"Rich says he's a good cop," Bernice persisted.

Time to fess up before her mother recited a list of eligible men from church or the nephews and grandsons of her Bunco friends. "I met a man. His name is Duke Dalton."

"Duke…? Is he from England?" Her mother chuckled at her own joke.

"I don't believe there are any members of the royal family living in Oklahoma. Duke moved here from Tulsa."

"An Okie."

"What do you know about Okies?"

"Dated one when I was a young gal."

Renée snapped her fingers. "I forgot your parents were migrant workers in Oklahoma before moving to Detroit."

"Daddy sure was excited to build cars. Life was good once he started putting on bumpers." Life had been better than good for many in Detroit before the downturn in the automotive industry.

"Duke owns a software company and he intends to knock down one of the warehouses along the Riverfront and erect a new building in its place." If Renée confessed the truth about why the warehouse needed to remain intact, her mother would volunteer to help and Bernice was too old to foster children anymore. "I can't go into detail, but I asked Duke to hold off demolishing the building for a week and he refused."

The knitting needles froze. "You're up to no good, aren't you, young lady?"

Even though Renée had the best of intentions, she had a history of becoming involved in situations that usually caused problems for her boss. She wiggled a finger into the tear in the couch cushion and protested, "Not at all."

"Then use your God-given gift to change his mind." Her mother believed all her daughter had to do was flash her dimples and others would gladly do her bidding.

"I tried," Renée muttered.

"And?"

"And he won't budge."

Bernice's expression softened. "Then you best leave well enough alone."

Not the advice Renée had hoped for.

Saved by the ringing doorbell, Renée bolted from the couch, pressed an eye to the peephole, then swallowed a groan and opened the door. "Hey, Rich."

The yellow glow of the porch light bounced off her brother's russet-colored hair, sparking a fireball above his head. Renée grinned. "It's Saturday night. Don't you have a date?" Like Officer Ben, her brother was divorced with no kids and always on the hunt for the next *Ms. Perfect.*

"Brat," he muttered, tugging a strand of her hair as he brushed past her into the room. "Hey, Mom."

"Hello, son." The needles clicked faster. Bernice was becoming agitated at having her quiet evening disturbed. "Imagine that, a visit from both children in one night."

Rich caught Renée's eye and nodded toward the kitchen.

"In the mood for ice cream?" Renée asked.

"Sure." He followed her out of the room.

"What's up?" she whispered, understanding full well why her brother had dropped in.

When she reached for an ice-cream bowl, Rich caught her wrist. "No, thanks." Her brother had been dieting since his fiftieth birthday, hoping to lose the extra ten pounds he'd put on over the years.

"What the hell were you thinking standing in front of that crane yesterday?"

"I was *thinking* I didn't want the building demolished."

"First, you asked me and Pete to increase our drive-bys along the Riverfront, then I discover you're interfering with a construction crew. What kind of trouble are you stirring up?"

He breathed deeply through his nose—a sign he was about to blow his lid. "Your nostrils are flaring," she teased.

"This isn't funny, especially if you're breaking the law."

"It's always about the law with you, isn't it?"

He scowled.

"I can't tell you, Rich. Not yet anyway. Promise you'll maintain your patrols a little while longer."

"Hell, Renée, if there were any criminals hanging around the Riverfront, they've all fled by now. The area's a graveyard." He crossed his arms over his chest. "If you're breaking the law, I risk losing my job for helping you."

"I'm bending, not breaking."

Her eyes must have conveyed sincerity, because he changed topics. "What did you and that Dalton guy discuss at the diner?"

"Mr. Dalton is relocating his computer software company from Tulsa to Detroit."

"And…?" Rich rested his palm against the butt of his gun.

Good grief. "The man didn't threaten me." At least not directly.

"Is he interested in dating you?"

"I'm going to pretend you didn't ask that question."

"C'mon, Renée. Mom's on my case every day of the week to find you a husband. There's a new cop at the precinct. He transferred in from Cleveland."

"No. No. And no." Every cop in Detroit knew Renée was Rich's little sister and most had heard the circumstances surrounding her adoption. The last person she intended to date or become serious with was a man who felt sorry for her. Too many damned people still treated her with kid gloves. Maybe that's what made Duke Dalton so intriguing. He wasn't from Detroit. He had no idea that she had a past. A very public past.

"Too bad. Dalton seemed okay." Rich peeked into the living room, then warned, "Stay away from that warehouse."

"But—"

"If you make trouble for Dalton, he'll lodge a complaint with the police department, then I'm caught in the middle."

The last thing she wished was to create problems for her brother. She'd have to find a way to stall Duke without resorting to drastic measures. Crossing her fingers, she followed her mother's suggestion and flashed her dimples. "I promise I won't get in the man's way."

LATE SUNDAY AFTERNOON—right in the middle of the Lions-Bears football game, Renée entered the Detroit Marriott. The hotel was located downtown in the General Motors Renaissance Center, which housed businesses, restaurants, bars, retail shops and a five-story atrium with river views. Across the street and accessible by a skywalk sat the Millender Center with additional stores and businesses.

Both the Renaissance Center and the Millender Center had station stops for Detroit's elevated light rail, the People Mover. The train traveled a three-mile loop around the area—not that Renée had much use for the mode of transportation in her line of work.

She rode the elevator to the hotel lobby on the third floor. Halfway to the front desk she changed her mind and backpedaled to the elevator bank. Rather than call ahead and notify Duke of her presence, she'd catch him off guard in his room. When it came to the corporate cowboy Renée needed every advantage.

Even though Duke's confidence and stubbornness irritated her, he was a man that stuck with a woman long after they'd gone separate ways. The sticking part had to do with his handsome face. But it had been the mellow glow in his dark brown eyes that had sucked her in like quicksand. Even if they worked out a solution to the Screw & Bolt Factory she and Duke were from different worlds and had nothing—save a little physical chemistry—in common.

Inside the elevator, she confirmed the number scrawled on the business card and punched the button for the sixty-second floor. In less than a minute she exited the elevator lightheaded from the slingshot ride. A few steps later she stood in front of Duke's door chewing her lip. When the coppery taste of blood met her tongue she swallowed a curse and rapped her knuckles against the wood.

"It's open. C'mon in," he called.

Had he been watching her through the peephole? Cautiously she turned the handle and entered the room, then gasped. Duke stood in front of a flat-screen TV wearing nothing but a white towel slung around his waist. Water from a recent shower dripped from his head and several droplets rolled down his smooth, hairless chest. Peeking out from beneath the terry cloth were masculine hairy calves and two big bare feet.

"Renée? What are you doing here?"

She forced her gaze from his chest to his face. It was four in the afternoon and he'd yet to shave. The dark stubble along his jaw added a swashbuckler element to his cowboy image, taking the guise to a whole new level of sexiness—a cowboy pirate.

The words *I'll return later* stuck to the sides of her throat, as she grappled for the doorknob.

"Wait." He stepped forward, the towel slipping to his hips. He clutched the knot at his waist and flashed a sheepish grin. "I was expecting room service. Make yourself comfortable while I dress." He retreated to the bathroom, leaving her a clear view of the unmade bed. A fantasy of her and Duke fooling around on the mattress was cut short by the sound of a throat clearing behind her.

A room-service waiter stood in the doorway. She stepped aside. The man rolled the cart past her and arranged service for two at the cocktail table in the corner, then left without pausing for a tip.

Drat. Duke had a date tonight. What rotten timing on her part.

Ignoring the zap of jealousy that pricked her at the idea of him and another woman enjoying a cozy meal and whatever else that followed, she decided to get right to the point.

Her attention rotated between the food, the football game and the bathroom door. Purely by accident her eyes landed on the bathroom door as Duke walked out, wearing jeans and a maroon turtleneck sweater. His big feet remained sock free and she forced her attention from his hairy toes—the whole bare feet thing impossibly intimate for having met the man two days ago.

He'd shaved. A sliver of disappointment pricked her as she studied his clean profile. He checked the game, then paused in front of her. *Eternity.* The subtle scent of the men's cologne enveloped her and she breathed deeply. Eternity for Men was one of her favorites. She'd given her brother a bottle for Christmas a year ago.

One side of Duke's mouth lifted and she caught

herself before responding to his smile. This was a business meeting, not a social call. "I didn't mean to interrupt—" she pointed to the table "—your dinner date."

He padded closer, his scent intensifying. In addition to cologne, her nose detected soap and shaving cream.

"I don't have a date," he said. "They always prepare the table for a guest. Will you join me?" He crossed the room, stopping on his way to straighten the bedcovers. "Sorry the place is a mess. I don't bother with maid service on the weekend." He held out a chair and waited.

The pull of his brown eyes tempted her to forget her mission. "I'm here to talk business."

"Share this pizza with me, then we'll discuss anything you want."

What could it hurt? Nothing but laundry and paperwork waited at home. She laid her coat across the end of the bed as she passed by and joined him at the table. He rewarded her with a sexy half smile and her heart flip-flopped inside her chest.

The man's lonely, that's all. He'd left family and friends behind in Tulsa. Maybe a lover. Well, Renée wasn't family. She doubted she'd leave today his friend. And becoming his lover…*dream on.*

He pushed her chair in after she sat. Duke had manners. Class. Style. She struggled to envision him mixing with Detroit's working-class. *And you'll never fit into his world.* Regardless, it was nice to pretend for a while that they had more in common than a crumbling warehouse.

"Are you a Lions fan?" she asked, as he poured two glasses of red wine, which probably cost as much as a week's worth of groceries.

"I intend to be." He served her a slice of pizza.

She sipped from her wineglass, waiting to see if he used silverware. He picked up the pizza slice with his fingers. His casual manner put her at ease. A bite later, she said, "This is delicious."

"Barbecue."

"An Oklahoma favorite?" she guessed.

"My stepfather's housekeeper's family recipe. I passed it along to the chefs in the kitchen. They loved it, so they added the pizza to the room-service menu."

A comfortable silence settled between them while they ate and watched the game. "Do you like football?" he asked when a commercial aired.

"Usually I don't have time to watch the games. Too busy responding to one crisis or another."

He stopped chewing. "You work seven days a week?"

"Sometimes. I'm on call Saturday and Sunday. Most of my coworkers are married and have families, so I cover weekend emergencies."

"You must rake in the overtime."

She shook her head. "I'm on salary, but the station wagon I drive is sort of a company car." Rich and several fellow officers at the precinct had organized a fund-raiser to purchase the car for Renée. People who had the least donated the most—as they always did when Detroit's Little Darling was involved.

"What's it like to pick up stakes and start over in a city where people don't recognize you?" She'd dreamed of doing that exact thing, but felt beholden to her mother and Rich for the blessed life they'd provided her. Now she was too entrenched in her job to ever consider leaving.

"Not as difficult as I'd imagined. I like Detroit." At her eye-roll he insisted, "There's a lot of energy here with the younger generation taking over the older neighborhoods and restoring them. I hope the Riverfront experiences the same revitalization sooner rather than later."

"Difficult to picture a cowboy fitting in with automotive workers."

"I'm not really a cowboy."

The rogue smile…the muscular body…the self-assured attitude…yeah, right. "So the boots and hat are for show?"

"The hat became a habit. And I told you the boots were a gift from my mother. She gave them to me shortly before she passed away, and you can't beat a sheepskin jacket in this bitter cold."

"I'm sorry about your mother."

"Ready to discuss the warehouse?" he asked, ignoring Renée's condolence. His mother must be a touchy subject.

"Let's not beat around the bush. I need you to hold off on the demolition for a week."

"Give me a reason."

Suddenly she lost her appetite and left the table to stand before the floor-to-ceiling windows at the end of the suite. The lights of Windsor, Ontario twinkled across the river. "Can't you trust me?"

"Trust you? I don't even *know* you." He joined her at the window, shoving his fingers through his dark hair, mussing the recently combed strands. "It's going to take a hell of a lot more than *trust me* to convince me to halt anything." When her gaze remained trained on Canada, he clasped her shoulder—his fingers firm, yet gentle. "Maybe I can help. I've got some pull with the—"

She stepped aside, breaking contact. The wealthy assumed they had the answer to every problem, when in fact, their interference usually made things worse. Right now she was battling a community development board comprised of local businessmen. She needed their approval for a recreation center for at-risk kids, which she hoped to open in the Warehouse District.

A year ago she'd acquired funding for the project and had approached the board for permission to purchase a deserted building that had once housed a dry cleaners and a food market. The board members denied her request citing that a center for *undesirable kids* would have a negative impact when they were trying to attract new businesses to the area.

For over a year Renée had worked tirelessly on the project, believing at-risk kids deserved a safe space to hang out and socialize after school. Instead, the children were left in the cold—like those she was attempting to assist now.

"What's it going to be, Renée?"

Dear God, she hoped she wasn't making the biggest mistake of her life. "I can't tell you. I'll have to show you."

Chapter Three

A night sky of sparkling stars greeted Renée and Duke when they left the hotel. "Maybe we should wait until tomorrow," he suggested. "It's dangerous along the Riverfront after dark."

"If you're concerned about safety, why are you moving your company there?" She marched toward the visitor parking lot.

Picking up his pace, Duke followed. "My office building will have surveillance cameras and a security guard 24/7."

"Not to worry. I doubt even criminals are foolish enough to venture out in these frigid temps."

The fact that Renée had grown up in Detroit and knew the area did nothing to ease his anxiety. "Should I follow you?"

"We'll take my car."

When they reached the wagon, he held open the driver-side door for her, then skirted the hood and hopped into the passenger seat. He fumbled with the lever then shoved the seat as far back as possible, which still left his knees pressed against the glove compartment.

She eyed his scrunched frame. "Would you rather drive your truck?"

"I'll manage as long as you don't slam on the brakes."

They made the short trip in silence. She turned into the Screw & Bolt Factory parking lot and drove past the construction crane to the far end where the gloomy outline of the building materialized. His muscles tightened with dread as he unfolded his long legs and got out of the car. A sixth sense warned he'd be better off never learning what Renée wanted with the warehouse.

"This way."

Duke walked at her side, his cowboy boots dragging across the brittle pavement. Hands fisted, his eyes fixated on the shadows, ready to protect Renée from whatever evil lay in wait.

As they drew closer to the building, he spotted the rusty sign: Industrial Public Warehouse. Renée paused to pull a flashlight from her coat pocket. She switched it on and they entered through a side service door. The yellow beam splashed across the chipped brick walls displaying the tags spray-painted by a local graffiti artist. Duke indicated the image of a bear-shaped man surrounded by smaller bear women. "The drawings are pretty good."

"I've encouraged Troy to apply to art school."

"You've met the kid who vandalized this property?" Duke's eyes prowled the area as they crossed the first floor. The popping and cracking of glass beneath their shoes echoed through the emptiness.

"Troy's nineteen. Doesn't have a job. Runs around with a group of troublemakers."

The kid should put his talent to better use than defacing public warehouses. Duke imagined his colleagues' astonishment if he commissioned the delinquent to sketch bears on the walls of the lobby in the new Dalton Industries building.

"Watch your step," she said as they entered a stairwell.

When they reached the third floor, light from the full moon spilled through a gaping hole in the wall, illuminating battered parts of thirty-year-old cars used for spray-painting practice. A skateboard ramp claimed the fourth floor. Someone had put in a lot of effort and time hauling large planks of plywood up four flights to construct the ramp.

They continued to the fifth and final floor. Duke and his Realtor hadn't bothered to investigate the top floor, assuming they'd find more of the same—debris and trash. She knocked on the door. Once. After a long pause she added two more knocks.

Was that a signal? What or who occupied the fifth floor?

Flashlight aimed in front of her, Renée opened the door.

Piles of newspapers and empty food containers littered the area. After several steps, she held up a hand and he stopped. The beam of light skirted across a maze of cardboard boxes that connected to form a tunnel. A towel concealed the opening at one end.

"It's me. Everyone okay in there?" Renée spoke in a hushed whisper.

Seconds ticked by and no sound. Finally a small hand pushed the towel aside and a face popped into view. A *kid's* face. Although the temperature in the building hovered below freezing, Duke's forehead broke out in a sweat. Images of a wrecking ball slamming into the side of the brick wall and children falling to their deaths flashed before his eyes.

One face turned into two. Three…four…*holy, hell.* A gang of kids had set up camp in *his* warehouse.

Renée ignored Duke's sharp indrawn breath, focusing on the children in front of her. "Hey, everyone. I brought a friend." Duke Dalton wasn't a friend by a long shot, but she didn't wish to frighten the children. Renée had discovered the clan a few days ago thanks to a tip from a transient woman in one of the city shelters. The elderly lady had overheard teenagers whispering about a group of kids hiding in a building along the Riverfront and had reported the news to shelter personnel.

The kids, save one, were familiar to Renée—most had been in and out of the foster-care system for years. Timmy, a shy, petite boy, slipped from the tunnel first. "Did you bring food?"

Oh, shoot. Guilt pricked her that she'd lounged in Duke's hotel room enjoying pizza while the kids had waited for supper—which she'd forgotten.

"Ms. Sweeney wanted to ask what everybody's hungry for." Duke's masculine voice sent Timmy scampering inside the tunnel.

Renée shot Duke a startled glance, surprised he'd come to her rescue. Flustered, she said, "Mr. Dalton won't hurt you."

Crystal, the Goth thirteen-year-old, emerged. Dressed from head-to-toe in black, she wore bell-bottom cargo pants with silver chains attached to the waistband, a T-shirt and clunky combat-style boots. Eyes rimmed with dark shadow and mascara, the teen had dyed her eyebrows and hair to match the ebony polish on her nails. Her menacing gaze fixated on Duke and she snarled, "Who's that?"

"This is Mr. Dalton. He's offered to buy supper tonight." When no one else came out, she said, "I need to make sure everyone is okay. If you don't come out, you don't eat."

"You heard Ms. Sweeney," Crystal called over her shoulder. "Hurry up. I'm starving."

One by one, five children crawled from the crude shelter. "José, where's your jacket?" The oldest in the group at fifteen, the boy jutted his chin defiantly. "It's hot in there."

"Well, it's not out here." She locked eyes with José, refusing to allow him to gain the upper hand. Thin and gangly, the shaggy-haired teen stood several inches taller than Renée. He had severe acne and she guessed his long bangs were meant to conceal the pimples across his forehead. After a tense few seconds he retrieved his coat.

Evie, Crystal's seven-year-old sister, shuffled forward. "Can I have milk tonight?" The cherub's cheeks glowed bright pink. Renée brushed aside a limp hank of blond hair and pressed her fingers to the child's forehead, relieved her skin felt cool. "Yes, you may have milk."

José exited the tunnel wearing a jacket with sleeves that ended above his bony wrists. She presumed he'd begun a growth spurt. The possibility frustrated Renée. The children shouldn't be living in cardboard boxes in an abandoned building with temperatures well below freezing at night. Every child was entitled to a warm bed and three square meals a day. Plus hugs. Kids needed hugs, which reminded her…she held out a hand toward Timmy. He hobbled closer, dragging his left foot behind him. The boy had been born with a clubfoot and had never received medical treatment for the deformity.

"Doing okay?" she asked, wrapping an arm around his shoulders. After the quick hug she directed the flashlight at Timmy's freckled face, searching for signs of injury, illness. He smiled, exposing a gap between his teeth.

"When did you lose your front tooth?"

"This morning. Ricci pulled it."

"Maybe Ricci should be a dentist when he grows up." Renée winked at the eight-year-old.

"No way," the boy protested. "I'm gonna race cars." She might have found his answer amusing if not for the fact that the Hispanic boy had been picked up twice by police for participating in illegal street racing. He'd been a passenger in the vehicles, but Renée feared one day Ricci would slide behind the wheel. If Renée didn't secure him a decent foster home soon, he'd end up in the state juvenile detention center before his twelfth birthday.

"I'm gonna fly airplanes," boasted Willie. Arms extended like wings, the six-year-old African American boy circled the group, making loud obnoxious engine noises. Willie was a crack baby. His cognitive development was a little slow, but not worrisome. It was his hyperactivity and emotional outbursts that had gotten him kicked out of every home he'd been sent to. Most foster parents weren't equipped to handle his behavioral issues.

While the kids engaged in good-natured bantering, Renée hugged each child in turn. She made sure they all felt the touch of a loving hand.

"Does that guy—" Crystal motioned to Duke "—have anything to do with the big crane we saw earlier?"

"Yes." She wouldn't lie to the children, but she refused to reveal the entire truth for fear the kids would panic and scatter. "Mr. Dalton owns this building."

The kids huddled close—José and Crystal standing guard in front of the younger ones.

Duke winced at the group's reaction and Renée wished to reassure him that he'd done nothing wrong. Street kids trusted no one. And even though she considered Duke's height and build, his square jaw and dark eyes attractive, the children no doubt found him formidable. "Mr. Dalton, I'd like you to meet your *temporary* tenants.

"This is José." To her pleasure, Duke extended his hand. To her displeasure José refused the handshake.

Ignoring the rebuff, Duke said, "Nice to meet you, José. Looks as if you're taking good care of everyone."

The boy's slim shoulders straightened, but the mutinous glare remained in his eyes. Renée wanted to hug Duke for complimenting the teen.

"This is Crystal and her sister, Evie."

Again Duke offered his hand. Crystal followed José's lead and kept her hands shoved inside her coat pockets. Evie giggled, burying her face in her sister's jacket.

"And our resident pilot is Willie." The boy marched over to Duke and shook his hand, pumping Duke's arm like a circus clown. "What's up, dude?" He laughed at his own joke.

"Hello, Willie." Duke didn't seem bothered by the rambunctious boy.

"Then we have Timmy and Ricci."

Ricci stayed put, but Timmy wandered closer, his twisted foot scraping against the cement. If Duke noticed the boy's deformity, he showed no sign.

"Nice to meet you, boys."

After the introductions, Timmy asked, "What are you gonna do to our building?"

Renée cringed at the word *our*.

"I intend to—"

"Mr. Dalton hasn't finalized his plans for the warehouse," she interrupted.

"We're not stupid," Crystal spouted. "You're gonna knock it down."

"Not yet," Renée assured the girl.

"Aw, man. Are we gonna have to find a new home?" Ricci whined.

Renée had been involved in social work too many

years to allow her emotions to get the best of her, but the fact that Ricci considered a vacant building a home made her eyes burn with anger—anger that these and many more kids had been left to fend for themselves by the system.

"You don't have to leave yet," she assured them.

Duke stirred uneasily and Renée regretted that she'd introduced him to the kids. But darn it, he'd forced her back to the wall. She had to prevent him from demolishing the warehouse while she attempted to line up foster homes for the children—not an easy job when the kids' files had been flagged as troublemakers.

"Are you and the others safe at night, José?" Duke asked, glancing at Renée.

She balled her hands into fists. Clearly the man believed she'd failed in her job as a social worker to meet the needs of these kids.

Haven't you, Renée? She blamed bureaucratic red tape for not being able to help all of Detroit's children in crisis. When a child slipped through the cracks, she asked herself if there was anything more she could have done. Had she missed details that might have made a difference in placing the kids in foster homes? She hated that Duke made her doubt herself. She'd only met him two days ago, but for some stupid reason the cowboy's opinion of her mattered.

"We're safe here," José mumbled. He looked at Renée before adding, "Two drunks sleep in the building next door, but they leave us alone." The teen indicated the Detroit United Railway Company powerhouse. The shell of a building would make an interesting view from the window of Duke's executive office.

"Glad to hear you're watching out for strangers," Duke said.

Crystal rolled her eyes. "We don't go out after dark."

Before the conversation lost its amicableness, Renée inquired, "How are you doing with supplies?" This past Wednesday when she'd discovered the group, she'd collected hand wipes, toilet paper, Kleenex, food and water.

She'd offered to escort the kids to a shelter to shower, but they'd refused, understanding that they'd be required to give their names and then be detained by the Department of Child and Family Services until an investigation into their situation had been conducted. These kids weren't new to the system.

"We need another blanket." José spoke up.

"Did one of the covers get ruined?" Renée had given them a car-trunkful of bedding from a local church.

"Not exactly." José's gaze skirted her face.

Renée deduced that the teen had traded the blanket for a pack of smokes. He had a habit of stealing from his foster homes and swapping the items for cigarettes. "Are you smoking again?"

"What if I am?" The words would have sounded more threatening if his pubescent voice hadn't cracked.

Renée narrowed her eyes, held out her hand and dared the teen to defy her. After a tense standoff, the teen withdrew an almost empty pack of cigarettes from his pants' pocket and handed it over. "Thank you." Then she spoke to the group. "What about breakfast foods and snacks?"

"We're good," Crystal answered.

The parishioners of Most Holy Trinity Church had donated granola bars, crackers, cookies and a bottle of chewable vitamins for the children. She hadn't dared leave the vitamins with the kids or they'd gobble them up like candy and become ill. She reached into her coat pocket and withdrew a bag filled with the animal-shaped supplements. "Hands out," she instructed, placing a tablet on each palm.

"Okay, then. Any last requests before Mr. Dalton and I fetch supper?"

Timmy raised his hand. "I finished my math problems."

"Bring me the workbook so I remember what level to get next time." A retired teacher in Renée's neighborhood had dropped off boxes of outdated math and reading materials to area shelters and Renée had confiscated a few for Timmy. "Anyone else need a workbook?"

A mini revolt erupted, and she laughed. "All right, all right." The last thing on these kids' minds was learning.

When Timmy handed over his work packet, Renée said, "This is fourth-grade level. I'm impressed." Out of all the kids, Timmy loved to learn. "I'll find you a fifth-grade level." She hugged each child again. Except José—he stepped aside, being too tough for affection.

"Stay safe and warm and—"

"Watch out for each other," Evie finished for her.

Renée waited until the kids crawled inside the cardboard tunnel. This was the most difficult part—leaving them behind. Then she felt Duke's hand on her elbow. Drat the man for his solicitous support—he was the enemy. In silence they navigated the stairwell to the first floor.

As soon as they exited the building he growled in her ear, "Why the hell are those kids living in my warehouse? And why the hell are you allowing them to?"

DUKE ESCORTED RENÉE to the station wagon, glancing over his shoulder, worrying that the drunks in the nearby building might follow them. Cold wind whipped his face, but red-hot anger melted the icy sting.

Gut clenched as if he'd been punched by the world's biggest bully, he forced his fingers to relax against Renée's arm lest he give in to the temptation to squeeze until he cut off her blood supply. He was on the verge of losing control—both terrifying and humiliating. He teetered on the rim of an emotional cliff unsure how to combat the surge of feelings assaulting him physically and mentally.

Fear. That the kids on the fifth floor might be dead right now if Renée hadn't arrived at the warehouse in time to prevent the wrecking ball from pummeling the brick walls. *Anger.* That Renée hadn't come clean with him Friday night at the diner. *Fury.* That the children had been deserted and left to fend for themselves like a pack of wild dogs. And lastly, *guilt* of all things. Tonight he'd sleep in a warm, clean bed while the kids on the fifth floor huddled together in a cardboard tunnel.

When they reached the car, he yanked open the driver's-side door for Renée, then crawled into the passenger seat. With new clarity, he appreciated the saying ignorance is bliss. Through the years, he'd read newspaper articles and viewed newscasts about the country's homeless. He accepted that these people inhabited the world. But until tonight they'd never been a part of *his* world.

"Duke?" The soft, shaky question snuck past his fury.

"I'm thinking," he snapped. Was he nuts? An idiot to believe he'd relocate his company to Detroit and the process would unfold without a hitch? He envisioned a new glass-and-steel structure replacing the old warehouse—an architectural showpiece standing tall and proud in the middle of blocks of rubble. Had he been so determined to escape his stepfather's shadow that he'd convinced himself *buying* that block of rubble was a wise decision?

"Are you okay?" Worry carved a line across Renée's forehead.

"No, I'm not okay." He clenched his hands into fists. "And you'd better not be okay with the kids living in those conditions." She jerked as if he'd slapped her.

Add remorse to the list of feelings gutting him.

"It's a long story." Her sigh reached inside his chest and yanked hard. "Sure you want to hear?"

"I don't have a choice, do I?"

She started the car and left the lot. As she navigated what little traffic there was on a Sunday night, he muttered, "I can't get their faces out of my mind." There was something terribly unconscionable about discarded children.

Duke had felt alone when his father had passed away, but he'd had his mother. She might not have spared much time for him, but at least she hadn't left him to fend for himself the way these children had been.

"I've seen more bad than good in my line of work," Renée said. "Believe me, there are worse dwellings for those kids."

"They shouldn't be allowed to stay there," he argued.

"They aren't being allowed." At his fierce scowl, she added, "There's a reason they're getting away with hiding out in a derelict building."

"I'm listening."

"The city doesn't have enough foster parents available on a continuous basis for kids in crisis. When a child is taken from a parent or found on the streets they often end up in city shelters while we investigate their situation and attempt to make permanent arrangements for them." She turned left at the corner and drove along a street lined with fast-food restaurants.

"The holidays are a difficult time to secure permanent care for kids. Most parents are already struggling to put gifts under the tree and a nice meal on the table. Many foster parents refuse to bring a troubled child into the mix during a time when families are supposed to rejoice and get along."

"Why not put the kids in a shelter until after Christmas? They'll freeze to death in this weather." Even though the children wore heavy coats, that didn't mean their toes and fingers weren't constantly numb.

"Shelters aren't safe for young children or teens."

"Better to take their chances there than die of hypothermia," he argued.

"Typical comment from someone who doesn't have a clue." Renée's fingers tightened until the knuckles turned white, and Duke figured she'd rather choke his neck than the steering wheel.

"Then give me a clue."

"Shelters are magnets for child predators and gangs. Kids risk getting raped, molested or beaten in them." She glanced across the seat. "You'd be wrong if you believed for a minute those children would rather stay in a shelter than out in the cold."

"Okay, so there are problems with a shelter, but those same problems exist on the streets. What if gang members discover the kids and harass them? Or those drunks who sleep next door suddenly pay a visit in the middle of the night? At least in a shelter they'd sleep on a bed instead of cold concrete. And they'd eat regular meals."

Renée didn't comment as she pulled into a drive-through restaurant and ordered eighteen tacos and twelve cartons of milk.

Duke pulled out his wallet. "I admit I grew up with advantages most kids only dream about." Even before his father had died and his mother had hooked up with her second husband, his family had lived in a nice home in an upper-middle-class neighborhood.

"Put your wallet away," she grumbled, digging through her purse.

"I insist." He doubted a social worker made enough money to feed herself let alone six kids. When Renée refused the two twenty-dollar bills he held out, he stuffed the cash into the purse on the seat between them. "At their age I was contemplating my next Little League game. Those kids worry over where their next meal's coming from."

"They're not starving to death." She drove forward to the order window and paid. "I'm doing my best to care for them until foster homes become available."

The bright lights of the restaurant flooded the car and Duke swallowed a curse at the unnatural sheen in her eyes. He'd been wrapped up in his own frustration and hadn't considered how difficult the situation was for Renée. Hell, if he was this upset after only meeting the kids once, he imagined how disturbing it was for Renée to interact with the children on a daily basis.

The pick-up window opened and Duke lost his chance to apologize. Renée set the bags of food on the seat, then drove off. "Tell me about the kids."

"Crystal and Evie are sisters," she began. "Their mother's been in prison the past two years and DCFS hasn't been successful in locating their father. Until a few months ago, the girls had been living with an aunt, but she became ill and was unable to care for them."

"And this DC…"

"DCFS—Department of Child and Family Services."

"Can't secure the girls a foster family?"

"We found a home for Evie. It's easier to place the younger ones. But Evie ran away when she learned her sister wasn't invited to go with her. Crystal lasted a day in a city shelter before she hit the streets. Luckily, a friend of Crystal's spotted Evie after she'd run off and took the little girl to where Crystal had been living with a group of kids in a city park."

Duke shuddered when he considered any of a hundred horrible fates the girls might have suffered. "What about the boy with the twisted foot?"

"Timmy's nine."

"You're kidding? I'd have guessed six. Maybe seven." But what did he know about kids?

"We're not supposed to have favorites, but Timmy's special." The warmth in her words suggested she possessed a soft spot for the boy. "He's been in foster care his entire life. His mother gave him up for adoption after his birth."

"Why isn't he in a home right now?"

"He was abused two years ago. Now he's a runner— takes off as soon as the foster parent turns their back."

"Timmy asked for a new workbook. Is he a smart kid?"

"He's an excellent student and loves to learn. But he's had a tough time in school. The other students pick on him."

What a waste. The boy was bright enough to succeed and overcome his physical deformity, but was denied the opportunity by a bunch of jerks.

"Ricci is eight. He hangs out with a street-racing gang most of the time. His mother's a methamphetamine user and we've attempted to get her help, but she hasn't cooperated. I believe Ricci's hanging out with the group because his mother's got a man staying with her. If both adults are doing drugs, Ricci's safer in the warehouse."

"How old is José?"

"Fifteen."

"What's his story?"

"He did time in a juvenile detention center for armed robbery—sort of."

"Sort of?"

"José held up a convenience store with a toy gun." She grimaced. "Finding him a foster home has been next to impossible. And if he goes into a shelter he'll end up joining a gang for protection."

Duke couldn't imagine any of the kids better off in a decaying pile of rubble. "That leaves the airplane pilot."

"Willie. He's six years old. Like Timmy he's been in and out of foster care his entire life. He has a few be-havioral issues that usually get him kicked out of the home after a while."

Renée drove along Atwater toward the river. "Now you understand why I need time."

He commiserated with the difficult position Renée was in and believed that she had the kids' best interests at heart. Yet his conscience demanded the children be removed from the building pronto—whether the demolition proceeded or not. Maybe if he forced her hand… "I'll give you until Tuesday to move the kids out."

"It's not a simple affair of escorting them off the premises."

Nothing involved with Renée Sweeney was simple. Two white teeth nibbled her lower lip. "What's wrong?" he pressed.

"I haven't told my boss about the children. No one but me and now you is aware they're living in the warehouse."

Great. Was she asking him to become her accomplice?

"If I report the kids as homeless, I'm required by law to bring them to a shelter or I risk losing my job."

Disbelief filled Duke.

Then she pleaded, "I promised I'd find them foster homes by Christmas."

"Christmas is three weeks away. Those kids need to be in a shelter *tonight*. They should have been in one from the beginning. My God, Renée, the crime rate in this area is off the charts."

"My brother and his partner are patrolling the area."

"The police are involved in your crazy scheme?"

"No," she gasped. "They have no idea why I've asked them to conduct drive-bys in the area."

"Trusting fellows," he muttered.

"All I'm asking is for you to hold off on your plans for the building a short while longer."

"No, you want me to ignore the fact that you're breaking the law."

Her eyes narrowed. "Don't you dare threaten me, Duke Dalton. Not unless you're prepared to accept the responsibility of your actions."

If not for the trembling of her lips, he would have assumed she found his warning meaningless. He admired her bravado, but allowing the kids to live in the building went against everything Duke believed right and morally responsible.

And a delay in demolition costs money you can't afford to lose.

She must have sensed he wouldn't waver. "The minute social services and the police show up at the warehouse, the kids will scatter. It's anybody's guess what horrors they'll have suffered by the time I find them."

Damn, Renée played dirty. If the children ran off and unthinkable things occurred, Duke would never forgive himself. *Give her a week, then you can walk away from the situation guilt free.*

After parking the wagon at the far end of the lot, she

left the motor running and the heat on. "Please, Duke." She grabbed his hand and squeezed—he felt her grip all the way to his heart. "Every child deserves to spend Christmas Eve in a warm bed and wake up in the morning to a gift under the tree. Help me make that happen for these kids."

No match for the pair of pretty blue eyes begging him, he caved. "One week. If they're not gone by then, I'm calling the cops."

Chapter Four

A shrill sound penetrated Duke's foggy brain.

Eyes shut, he slapped a hand along the nightstand until his fingers bumped his cell phone. After a few seconds of fumbling he grumped, "Dalton."

"It's 9:00 a.m.," the caller accused. "Why are you still in…oops. Do you have an overnight guest with you?"

I wish. "Sorry to disappoint you, Sam. I'm all by my lonesome in bed." Duke loved his younger stepsister, but at the moment he was tempted to hang up on her. She'd pestered him earlier in the week about spending Christmas at the ranch, but he'd been hesitant to commit. No way was he leaving Detroit until Renée resolved the situation with the kids in the warehouse.

"Hang on," he muttered. After a full-body stretch, he shoved himself into an upright position against the headboard. "Okay. I'm awake."

Sam droned on about the holidays, but he paid little attention, his mind reliving the previous night's dream—him kissing Renée. Him removing her clothes. Him tonguing those cute little dimples in her cheeks. What he wouldn't give to have the social worker cuddled next to him in bed right now. His musings turned X-rated as he imagined their bodies, slick with sweat, rubbing—

"Duke!"

"Ouch." He held the phone away from his ear.

"Sorry. I thought you'd drifted off. Are you sick? Need me to fly up and take care of you?" Sam was the type of person who'd drop everything in her world to come to someone's rescue. Both his stepsister and Renée possessed a soft heart.

"I'm fine, Sam." When Duke and his mother had first arrived at the Cartwright ranch in Oklahoma, Sam had been ten. Angry at having to leave his friends and school, Duke had wanted nothing to do with his new family or the ranch. Then Sam had latched on to him like a lost puppy. As much as she'd been a nuisance, he'd been grateful for the attention, because his mother had been more concerned with winning over her stepchildren and pleasing her new husband than spending time with her grieving son.

"How are the plans progressing for the new building?" Sam asked, dragging his mind from the past.

"There's been a delay in the demolition."

"Nothing serious, I hope."

Six homeless kids squatting on the property was about as serious as serious got. He steered the topic in another direction. "How's everyone at home?"

"Matt's got another crazy scheme up his sleeve. He plans to start a horse-breeding operation."

"What kind of horses?"

"Cutting horses."

Younger than Duke by one year, Matt Cartwright was cowboy through and through—stubborn and impulsive. He often acted without considering the consequences, and there was no changing the man's mind once he set course. Duke admired his stepbrother's fearless attitude. There were times when Duke was too cautious and he'd lost business opportunities because he'd overanalyzed the situation. Case in point—his current quandary. If he'd gone with the first and more expensive demolition bid rather than seek additional quotes, the warehouse would have been reduced to a pile of rubble weeks ago—before the homeless kids had commandeered the building.

For most of his twenties and into his thirties, Matt had enjoyed a successful rodeo career as a tie-down roper. At thirty-four, he was considered one of the top competitors in the Prairie Circuit—Nebraska, Kansas and Oklahoma. This past November he'd won the Prairie Circuit Finals Rodeo in Guthrie, Oklahoma. "What does Dominick say about Matt's plans?"

A giggle filtered through the earpiece. "Daddy believes horses are a waste of time and money."

Sounds like Dominick. Matt would have his hands full convincing his father to bankroll his latest venture—unlike Duke, who'd declined the man's offer to invest in Dalton Industries. "Sorry, Sam, but I'm not up to refereeing this latest match between Matt and your father."

"It's almost Christmas, Duke. You don't want to spend the holidays alone in Detroit. Juanita promises to cook your favorite dishes if you fly home."

Saliva flooded his mouth. The Cartwright housekeeper had been a permanent fixture on the Lazy River Ranch since Sam and Matt's mother had deserted the family when they were toddlers. "I can't make any promises. I've got to straighten out this latest mess or the entire project faces more delays."

"Okay, then I'll spend Christmas with you. I've never been to Detroit. And it would be fun to shop in Canada."

Shopping with Sam—no. The woman had feet of

steel—capable of logging fifty miles of mall walking before she quit for the day. "Sam, what's really bothering you?" He sensed there was more to his stepsister's calls than wishing Duke home for the holidays.

A pause. Then a sigh. "I'm bored," she confessed. "So damned bored I'm going out of my mind."

"I'm listening."

"I've had it with this nine-to-five job Daddy created to keep tabs on me."

Duke sympathized with both Sam and his stepfather. When Sam had been sixteen, she'd almost died as a result of a kick to the head by a horse. From that day forward Dominick had treated his daughter with kid gloves, never allowing her to venture too far out of sight or mind. Because of the injury, Sam suffered occasional memory lapses and poor concentration. As the years passed, Sam matured and learned to manage her shortcomings. But Dominick had issues with letting go. He'd created a marketing position at Cartwright Oil for Sam, hoping she'd feel useful and needed. In reality, the old man had created a prison and tossed his daughter inside.

"Quit," Duke suggested.

"Then what am I going to do?" Duke heard Sam sniff.

Oh, hell. He couldn't deal with tears. "Why don't you fly up the weekend before Christmas."

"You mean that? I can come to Detroit?"

"Yes, you can visit me, brat."

"I won't tell Daddy my plans until right before I leave, then he can't stop me."

Duke grimaced. He was sure to earn a spot on his stepfather's most-wanted list for aiding and abetting Sam's escape. "I better go."

"Duke, wait."

"What?"

"You're the best. Love you. Bye." Sam hung up and he tossed his phone on the bed.

The best? He didn't feel like the best.

He swung his legs to the side of the bed and sat.

Wednesday.

If he spent another day in the room, monitoring non-existent e-mails and phone messages he'd go crazy. December was a slow month for his company. He'd been in contact with his managers in Tulsa every day, but nothing needed his attention. And he certainly didn't care to share with his top executives that his plans for the new building had been derailed by a bunch of vagrant children.

At Renée's request he'd agreed not to return to the warehouse for fear he'd scare the kids and they'd run off. But their sad little faces remained in his mind. Sunday night after they'd delivered the tacos to the group, he'd lain in his hotel-room bed, worrying if the children were cold. Scared. Lonely.

He hadn't had a decent night's sleep since and he doubted he'd experience another one until each runaway had been placed in a foster home. He'd expected an update from Renée by now, but had heard nothing. Maybe he'd drop by her office to ensure she didn't fall victim to the out-of-sight-out-of-mind phenomenon.

OH. MY. GOD.

What was he doing here?

Renée sat at her desk in the Department of Child and Family Services, having just finished conducting a phone interview with a potential foster parent when Duke Dalton waltzed through the door. Every female in the room ogled the cowboy—all six-foot-something of him, sporting a cowboy hat, sheepskin coat and those ridiculous snakeskin boots. Duke had yet to spot her, as he scanned the crowded room of desks covered with files and coffee mugs. Renée's heart pounded, not from fear or worry—from excitement. Her insides had gone all jittery at the sight of a man who represented nothing but trouble for her—how crazy was that?

"What's the meaning of this?"

Startled, she spun in her seat and swallowed a groan at the stern expression on her boss's face. Harriet Kromyer had been head of the department years before Renée had arrived. Nicknamed the Iron Bat, Harriet's hair was the color of aged steel and she wore it in a tight bun, which emphasized her huge bat ears. "What's what?" Renée asked.

A file folder landed with a *smack* on the desk. "What happened to locating a new foster home for Benjamin Reynolds? Mrs. O'Brien phoned, claiming you'd promised to pick up the boy two days ago."

Drat. Renée had forgotten all about her agreement with Mrs. O'Brien. "I haven't been able to place Benjamin anywhere." The poor child had been relegated to the bottom of Renée's to-do list when she'd discovered the kids in the warehouse.

"Then follow proper procedure and drop the boy off at a shelter until a home becomes available," her boss said with a frown.

"I'll phone Mrs. O'Brien right away and apologize." A tingle attacked Renée's neck and she worried that Duke's wandering gaze had discovered her.

Harriet's upper lip curled. "Never mind calling. Get over there and collect the boy today."

Renée swallowed a sigh of impatience. After almost nine years in the department Harriet barely tolerated Renée's presence. Unbeknownst to her coworkers,

Renée and her boss shared one commonality—they'd both been abandoned children. But that's where the similarities ended. Unlike Renée, Harriet had spent her childhood bouncing from one foster home to another, while Renée had been fortunate to get adopted. She suspected Harriet resented the media attention Renée's abandonment case had received while Harriet's experience had gathered no interest.

"Excuse me." Duke interrupted the conversation, his voice husky and intimate. The skin on Renée's arms erupted in tiny goose pimples.

Harriet's mouth gaped, the silver fillings in her lower teeth sparkling under the fluorescent lights. "May I—" she cleared her throat "—help you?"

"Duke Dalton."

"Nice to meet you, Mr. Dalton. Harriet Kromyer, head of DCFS." Her boss stood straighter and offered a smile, which she rarely imparted to her employees.

"I'm staying at the Detroit Marriott and I've noticed a couple of kids hanging out in a nearby neighborhood whom I believe might be homeless. The hotel manager suggested I contact your department."

Alarm bells tolled inside Renée. She was still on probation for her most recent act of defiance and the Iron Bat would love nothing more than to suspend Renée. Renée doubted she'd ever be forgiven for embarrassing Harriet and the department when Renée had used her popularity with the media to draw attention to an injustice committed by the district attorney this past fall.

In her opinion, the schmuck had deserved to be raked over the proverbial coals by the local press. The attorney and his wife had taken in a foster child for the sole purpose of appearing sympathetic to voters. As soon as the attorney had been elected to his new post he'd dropped off the boy at DCFS citing behavioral and psychological problems with the child.

Renée had been so furious she'd called a newspaper reporter she'd become friends with. The reporter ran a story that spawned a public outcry and calls for the attorney's resignation. When Harriet had discovered Renée had leaked the information to the press, she'd been furious.

Any other DCFS employee would have been fired on the spot, but Renée's history with the media and the fact that she'd earned a reputation as a champion for Detroit's needy children prevented Harriet from getting rid of her. Regardless of her past actions, Renée couldn't afford a suspension—not when the kids living in the warehouse were depending on her to pull off a Christmas miracle.

"I'd appreciate it if an employee in your department would investigate the kids," Duke spoke, interrupting Renée's musings.

"This is Ms. Sweeney…Detroit's Little Darling. She'll be happy to investigate the situation." Harriet turned to Renée. "I want a report on my desk tomorrow."

As soon as the boss's office door closed, Duke flashed a sexy half grin that would have turned Renée's knees to putty if she'd been standing. "What are you doing here?" she whispered, aware of her coworkers observing them.

"Can we speak in private?"

She glanced at the wall clock. Almost noon. "I've got time for a quick lunch." She grabbed the duffel bag of folders, phone lists and additional junk she hauled around with her, then stuffed Benjamin Reynolds's file inside and reached for her coat draped across the chair.

Pressing a hand to her lower back, Duke escorted her through the maze of desks. They were halfway to the door when she feared the heat from his fingers might singe the feathers inside her down jacket.

In the hallway, she skirted his touch. "Don't you have a business to run?"

"With the demolition on hold, I'm at loose ends this week."

They stepped into an empty elevator, the small chamber quickly filling with the scent of Duke's cologne. His probing stare caused her heart to beat out of whack. "What?" she asked, when he continued gawking.

One side—always the right side—of his mouth curved upward. The half smile plus his heavy-lidded gaze lent the cowboy way too much sex appeal.

"I like looking at you," he admitted. "You're a very attractive woman."

Thank God the elevator doors opened. With brisk steps, she crossed the lobby. Her dreams of Duke the past few days hadn't done the man justice. She swore his eyes had been plain brown, not a warm, rich dark chocolate. And she remembered he was tall—but had her head really only come to his shoulder? And that darned voice—rumbling like a well-tuned Corvette.

When they exited the building, she spoke. "Where are you parked?"

"Across the street." He led the way to his truck. Once they buckled up and he'd turned the key, she ripped into him.

"Are you crazy? Why in the world would you show up at the department?"

"Why did she call you Detroit's Little Darling?" he countered.

Feeling as if a boulder had been tossed in her path, her anger stumbled. If she had her way, Duke would never learn the circumstance behind the nickname. "It's a long story. Suffice it to say, I'm Harriet's least favorite employee."

He seemed to accept her answer because he asked, "What are you hungry for?" Then he pulled away from the curb and merged with traffic.

"There's a café a few blocks from here. Take a right at the next light."

"How are the kids?"

"They're fine. I've lined up a home for Evie. I'm waiting to hear if they'll accept Crystal."

"Why wouldn't they?"

"They're already fostering four other children."

"Four?"

"The kids living with the Jensens are well-behaved and I don't believe the sisters will give the couple any trouble." At least she hoped not. "Mrs. Jensen wants to take the girls, but Mr. Jensen is reluctant to because his wife has a few medical issues and he's worried that caring for six children will be too much for her."

"What are the chances of Mr. Jensen giving in to his wife?"

"Fifty-fifty. I'm meeting with him this afternoon." Mr. Jensen was a postal carrier and she intended to accompany him on his route with the hope of convincing him that Crystal would be a big help to his wife with the cleaning and cooking.

Duke turned at the light. "I'd be happy to tag along."

"Thanks, but I don't want Mr. Jensen to feel ganged up on." After another block, she pointed out the windshield. "The restaurant's on the left. There's parking in the lot next door."

Mammy's Café butted up to a residential neighborhood. They dashed across the busy street and found themselves packed like sardines in the noisy waiting area. Renée rose on tiptoe to ask if Duke wanted to try a different restaurant when he lowered his head, accidentally brushing his ear against her mouth. She jerked at the jolt that zapped her lips.

"Renée!" A woman in her early fifties weaved through the crowd. "You haven't been by in a couple of weeks."

"Busy with work." Renée hugged the rotund woman. "May, this is Duke Dalton. Duke this is May. She owns Mammy's."

A pencil-thin eyebrow arched, as May took in Duke head to toe before motioning to his hat. "Are you a real cowboy?"

Duke's laughter drew stares and Renée felt her face warm. "No," he answered. "I just like the clothes."

"Well, the clothes like you. C'mon. I'll seat you near the kitchen."

Several patrons recognized Renée and waved. She did her best to act as if all was well when in truth her everyday world was on the verge of imploding and Duke Dalton was the lit stick of dynamite set to make it blow.

Once they reached the table, May asked, "The usual?"

"Reuben on toasted wheat with coleslaw and a cup of French onion soup," Renée explained for Duke's benefit.

"Make mine the same." Then he added, "I'll have coffee when you get the chance."

Renée waved off the coffee question in May's eyes. "Water's fine."

Left alone, Duke murmured, "Hanging out with Detroit's Little Darling has its advantages."

Yes, Renée was popular all right, thanks to the circumstances that had surrounded her birth. Now that she was thirty-one, the younger generation often didn't recognize her, but older folks did. They stopped her on the street and asked about her past, which always surprised

Renée. What person remembers being born let alone their first few years?

"Here ya go, cowboy." May slid a coffee mug in front of Duke and a water glass by Renée. "Food will be up shortly."

"We talked about Crystal and Evie." He sipped his coffee, eyes squinting above the steam rising from the mug. "What about the others?"

"No luck so far." Renée hated admitting defeat.

"Is anyone helping you search for foster homes?"

"I'm on my own." She didn't dare ask others to involve themselves in a situation that wasn't by-the-book. It was enough that her own job was on the line. "My coworkers have more than their share of case loads. We're understaffed and overworked—typical for large cities such as Detroit."

"Did Timmy get the new workbook he asked for?"

Duke remembered. "I dropped off a few math packets Monday night."

His brow furrowed. "It isn't safe along the Riverfront after dark. Next time I'll go with you."

Surprised by Duke's concern, Renée defended herself. "I carry mace and I have my cell phone with me at all times." Not that either would do any good if a man Duke's size jumped her in the dark. For the most part she relied on intuition and common sense to stay safe.

May delivered their meals and for a few minutes Renée and Duke enjoyed their sandwiches and soup. "This is excellent," he said between bites. "I'll have to remember this café."

"Most wealthy people aren't adventurous enough to wander into the older sections of Detroit. If they were, they'd discover an abundance of mom-and-pop restaurants that serve terrific ethnic food."

"You sure have a chip on your shoulder when it comes to the rich."

Shoot. She should have kept her mouth shut but she'd dropped her guard—probably because Duke didn't act like the well-to-do people she'd come in contact with through her job. If she wasn't careful, she'd be tempted to trust the man. "Back to your surprise visit to the DCFS—were you curious about the kids in the warehouse or did you want to speak to me about another issue?"

"I've been thinking."

Oh, dear.

"Since I'm stuck for the rest of the week with nothing to do I'd—"

"No."

He stared.

"You can't get involved, Duke. Consider your company's reputation. You don't want the public to discover you were aware of the kids on your property, but didn't report them to the police."

"I reported them to *you,*" he protested. "And for the record, I'm not worried about my reputation."

Sure. Personal experience had taught Renée that most people obsessed over their good names. Wasn't that why her birth mother had done the unthinkable?

"I want to help, and the kids deserve a little fun. The Red Wings are in town tomorrow. I got a great deal on eight tickets from the hotel manager. We can pick up the kids at the warehouse and bring them to the hotel, then ride the People Mover over to the Joe Louis Arena. I'll treat everyone to supper at the hockey game."

That Duke wanted to show the children a good time shook Renée to the core. She dreamed of having the extra money to take kids in crisis on field trips, where for a short while they'd forget their ugly lives and have fun.

"C'mon, Renée." He rested his hand atop her drumming fingers, halting the *click, click, click* of her nails against the table. "This may be the last time they have fun together before they're split up."

"They don't trust you, Duke. I'll never be able to talk them into leaving the warehouse."

"They trust you, don't they?"

The younger children trusted Renée, but Crystal and José were older and wouldn't be as easy to sway. The teens had seen and experienced too many bad things in their lives and assumed all adults had ulterior motives. But Duke was right. The group needed an activity that would relieve the stress and tension of their daily existence. And what about her? It had been a long time since she'd done anything fun.

With a handsome man.

She'd yet to decide when Duke leaned across the table and whispered, "You've been on my mind a lot, Renée. I'd like to get to know you better."

She inhaled deeply, suddenly feeling lightheaded.

"It's the perfect date," he continued. "The kids have fun and we get to spend time together."

The warmth in his brown eyes defeated her. "Okay. I'll see if the kids want to go. But on one condition." She told herself that the only reason she agreed to the outing was because she hadn't the heart to deny the children an experience of a lifetime.

"What condition?"

"It's not a real date."

Eyes wide, he asked, "You want to go out on a pretend date?"

Ha. Ha. "I don't want to date at all."

He flashed a we'll-see-about-that grin.

Chapter Five

"Wow, this is cool," Ricci said, switching seats with Timmy for the fifth time.

Duke and Renée had herded the children onto the light rail train at the Renaissance Center. Most days the People Mover wasn't crowded, but a Red Wings game brought in fans from out of town, packing the train car. Duke wasn't sure if the kids' excitement or Renée's presence was responsible for the attention they drew from other passengers. He wished he understood what caused complete strangers to call out her name or stop to speak with her. Several riders recognized Renée but the blank expression on her face testified that she'd never met them previously.

Before he had an opportunity to further ponder the social worker's popularity, Timmy pointed to the cars parked on the street below the rail. "Willie, we're flying."

Nose pressed to the window, Willie shouted, "Watch out! We're gonna crash!" His comment drew concerned glances from the riders. Renée caught the boy's attention and pressed a finger to her mouth signaling him to be quiet.

The train traveled on a single track through a one-way loop around the downtown central business district.

Duke's Realtor had explained that the funding to expand the mass transit project had dried up after Jimmy Carter lost his bid for a second term in the White House.

José sat two seats away. The teen wasn't impressed with the light rail system. Dark brown eyes roamed from person to person, as if anticipating an ambush— his edgy behavior likely the result of doing time in a juvie facility. According to Renée the kid had resisted the lure of gangs, but for how long? When would José give in and pledge allegiance to a group of thugs for protection and camaraderie? The idea that the young man had few choices in life bothered Duke more than he cared to admit.

A pat on his knee caught his attention. The blond girl, Evie, stood before him, her arms raised above her head, gray eyes beseeching. He hesitated, his gaze seeking Renée, but she and Crystal were deep in conversation. Surprised Evie trusted him after only meeting him a few days ago, Duke set her on his lap and she burrowed into his jacket.

His chest tightened, generating a dull throb that grew in intensity with each passing second. He wouldn't allow himself to question the child's behavior because that would lead to contemplating how few times the little girl had been held or cuddled in her short life. What he did find troubling was Evie's innocent acceptance of strangers—yet who else was she to turn to in a time of crisis? When you lived on the street, everyone was a stranger. He tightened his arms around the fragile shoulders, ignoring the smell of oily hair, dirty clothes and the sting of her ankle-high boots clunking his shins. The shoes were too large for her small feet, as were the dirty pink mittens she rested her cheek against.

All the kids needed a good scrubbing and their

clothes laundered. What an odd group they made—a well-groomed couple traveling with a bunch of grubby kids and Crystal—who resembled the Devil's sidekick.

Pushing his way between two standing passengers, Willie searched for an open window to stare out. Fearing expulsion from the train, Duke called, "Willie, come here." The boy stopped in front of Duke and stared at Evie, who'd dozed off. Instinctively Duke tightened his hold on the child. He predicted the girl's sleeping habits were a succession of catnaps—hunger, cold and fear preventing her from succumbing to deep, peaceful slumber. He patted his available thigh. "Sit right here, Willie. You'll have a better view of the lights outside."

Willie pounced on the adult-size leg, eliciting an *oomph* from Duke. The boy swayed precariously and Duke grabbed his jacket to prevent him from toppling to the floor, then held him steady with an arm around his small waist.

A few minutes later—about the time Duke's lower appendages had gone numb—the driverless train pulled into the Joe Louis Arena Station, and Renée gathered the children into a group. Duke carried a sleeping Evie and held Willie's hand, fearing the kid would fly off and become swallowed by the crowd.

Once they entered the station, they stood to the side, allowing the throng of people to disperse. José studied the two Venetian glass mosaics hanging on the wall across from the train. The other kids joined him, their gazes glued to the pieces of bright orange glass. Each of the thirteen stations along the People Mover route displayed original artwork.

"The artist's name is Mr. Kamrowski." Renée pointed to the nameplate.

"What's it supposed to be?" Crystal asked.

"A group of astrological and mythological figures from the seventeenth century." Renée indicated the half animal, half human figure to one side of the design.

"Cool," Ricci praised.

When Duke noticed José's interest in the artwork, he added, "There's a brochure on this piece in my hotel room. The artist originally used blue to depict the sky because the images are those of constellations."

José shifted, putting more space between him and Duke. "Then how come it's all orange?"

"Someone decided orange suited the colors in the arena."

"Blue would have been better." José traced a finger along one of the glass pieces.

"How do they make this stuff?" Timmy asked.

"The artist drew a mural, then sent the picture to a small town in Italy called Spillemberg. There, stained-glass workers pounded out small pieces of colored glass and glued each one to sheets of paper marked with the design. When they finished, they shipped it here and had the panels installed in the station walls."

"Everyone hungry?" Renée spoke.

A chorus of "Yeahs" erupted.

"We're sitting in section 114. Why don't we grab dinner at that end of the arena," Duke suggested.

"Your arm is probably numb." Renée nodded at Evie. "I'll hold her for a while."

"I'm fine. Our seats aren't far." Duke was impressed with Renée's ability to monitor the kids along the crowded concourse. Like a sheepdog, she veered right, then left, never allowing one child to wander too far from the group. The concession stand was an experience Duke wasn't likely to forget.

Six pairs of eyes bulged at the array of food choices.

Orders were shouted and minds changed at alarming speed. Finally Duke rescued the frazzled food-service employee and shooed the kids off to wait with Renée against the far wall. He ordered eight Little Caesars pepperoni pizzas, extra hot dogs, fries, nachos and drinks. Then he offered the employee a twenty-five dollar tip to deliver the order. He rejoined the group. "Let's find our seats while we wait for our meals." They filed past the red privacy curtain and into the arena.

"Aw, man, this is way cool!" Ricci exclaimed, his gaze shooting around the twelve-million foot facility.

"Better than street racing?" Duke teased.

"Hell, no!" the boy shouted.

"Ricci, watch your language." Renée snagged Duke's coat sleeve when they reached the seats and whispered, "How much did the tickets cost?"

"Don't worry." Duke had paid half the value of the tickets because the season-tickets holders were out of town. Not that six hundred dollars was a bargain, but witnessing the kids' faces light with excitement was worth every penny. Their section offered a view most fans only dreamed of—right behind the glass.

Add the cost of food and souvenirs, which he'd yet to buy and tonight's tab would run him close to a thousand dollars. He didn't plan to tell Renée about the gifts for the kids because he figured she'd balk at spending more money. But he'd witnessed the yearning on their faces as they'd strolled past the Hockey Town Athletics store. The fact that not one of them had begged for anything made Duke sad. They'd probably been told "No" so many times in their young lives that they'd quit asking.

While the kids stood in front of the safety glass watching the teams warm up, Duke sat and shifted Evie in his lap. Circulation restored to his arm, he winced at the painful pinpricks attacking the muscle.

Renée leaned closer. "I'll pay for half the tickets."

Time to lie. "I got the tickets for free, Renée." Her eyebrows came together in a cute glower. "The hotel manager is friends with the season-tickets holder and they're out of town tonight." Partially true. No way would he take her money.

"At least allow me to cover my ticket and meal."

"Why? So you can't call this a date?"

"This isn't a date." She pursed her lips. Cute *and* determined—a dangerous combination.

Before they began an argument, two arena workers arrived, their arms loaded with food bags and drinks. Renée took charge, directing everyone to their seats and distributing the food. Duke jiggled Evie awake. The little girl's sleepy smile went straight to his heart. He settled her in the chair between him and Renée and she tore into her pizza, eyes wide as she observed the sights and sounds around her.

A half hour later team warm-ups ended and the Zamboni machine appeared. Once again the kids rushed to the glass to watch the machine resurface the ice.

Duke turned his attention to Renée. "Do you attend Red Wings games very often?"

"I went to a few when I was younger, but the ticket prices are outrageous nowadays."

"That's because the Red Wings are one of the best teams in the Western Conference. They sell out every game."

"Since when does an Oklahoma cowboy know so much about a Detroit hockey team?" Dimples accompanied the question and Duke lost his train of thought as he stared at the tempting pits.

When she patted his arm, he jumped. "I'm sorry, what was that?" he asked stupidly. Another smile. More dimples. Duke was falling fast and hard.

"Never mind," she muttered, eyes sparkling with humor.

"What do you do in your spare time?" he asked, trying to snap out of the spell she held over him.

"Catch up on sleep, do laundry and run errands."

"Exciting."

"What do you do when you're not working?" she countered.

"Now that I'm living near water, I intend to buy a boat and teach myself how to fish."

"The only outdoor sport I enjoy is ice skating. My neighborhood park has a fishing pond that freezes over and I lace up the skates once or twice a year."

"I've never skated. Want to teach me how?" He swallowed a groan when her face reddened. Obviously his man-on-the-make skills needed fine-tuning. He'd been out of the dating scene over a year—since he'd broken things off with his almost-fiancée.

Elizabeth was an up-and-coming lawyer in Tulsa, working toward a partnership in her firm. A pretty brunette, he'd fallen head over heels in love with her energy and sharp wit. Six months after they'd begun dating he'd purchased an engagement ring. Because Elizabeth worked long hours, Duke had scheduled a dinner with her two weeks in advance at an upscale restaurant in Tulsa, where he'd planned to propose. In his best suit and tie, he'd waited at the restaurant. Elizabeth hadn't showed. He'd called her cell phone and her office phone, but had gotten her voice mail. Then he'd paged her. Nothing. Texted her. Nothing. After waiting two hours he'd finally left.

When Elizabeth had contacted him the next day he'd had to remind her that she'd forgotten their date. Her clipped apology before rushing off to a meeting had convinced Duke that she'd always put her job first before him. He'd broken off the relationship, worrying that he'd never find a woman who'd put him first in her life.

"I'm not sure a man of your height should wear skates. If you fall, it's a long way to the ground," Renée joked.

He chuckled, but his mind wasn't on skating. What was it about Renée Sweeney that intrigued him—aside from her cute smile and the fact that inside the petite social worker beat the heart of a gladiator: fearless and determined.

Even though he admired her for championing the kids who lived in Detroit's trenches, Duke warned himself to steer clear of a serious relationship with her. Like his mother and his former girlfriend, Renée had no time for him. Would friendship be enough with Renée or would he always want more?

The arena horn blasted and the kids claimed their seats. The players were introduced and the game commenced. Tracking the puck's movement across the ice proved a challenge for even the most devoted fan. The kids didn't care. They were caught up in the excitement of the noisy crowd and players slamming into the glass in front of them.

At the beginning of the third period, Renée, Crystal and Evie left for the ladies' room. Then Duke herded the boys to the men's room. After he escorted them to their section, he snuck out to the concourse and purchased souvenirs. Bobblehead dolls for the boys. Red Wings pillows for the girls. Red Wings backpacks for everyone. And a jersey for Renée. He wanted her to have a keepsake of tonight's outing.

Arms loaded with bags, and licorice ropes he returned to their section during a break in the action. The kids offered him a reception Santa Claus would have been envious of. Renée did her best to restore order but Willie refused to stay in his seat and José yelled at Ricci to quit stepping on his toes. The fans around them didn't appear disturbed by the commotion and smiled at the kids' excitement.

Renée gasped when Duke handed her the jersey. An inebriated man shouted, "Give him a thank-you kiss, lady!" Renée blushed profusely, ignoring the "kiss him, kiss him, kiss him" chant growing in volume. Then the kids got into the act and urged Renée to wear the jersey, which she pulled over her sweater. Duke's mind conjured up an image of her wearing the shirt with nothing but her birthday suit beneath.

Still daydreaming, he wasn't prepared when she leaned across the chair and planted a big smack on his cheek. Suddenly the temperature inside the arena spiked—hot enough to melt ice.

"Thank you, Duke," she whispered.

A round of applause accompanied by whoops and hollers broke out, then the crowd quieted and the kids fiddled with their souvenirs. After the final buzzer sounded the Red Wings skated off the ice with another victory. For a few hours he'd made six kids happy and he'd received his first kiss from Renée.

Life didn't get much better than this.

For friends.

SEATED ON THE PEOPLE MOVER once again, Renée studied an exhausted Duke. Eyes closed, he slouched in his chair, his head lolling side to side with the sway of the train. She wanted to kiss him again for giving the children this fairy-tale evening. Renée had never seen anything so sweet as when Evie left her seat, crawled onto Duke's lap and snuggled into a ball. Automatically his arms cradled the child.

Timmy wiggled close, resting his head against Duke's shoulder. Ricci and Willie lay sprawled across two seats sleeping. Tonight, Renée hoped their dreams would be filled with bobbleheads, licorice ropes and hockey players.

The two teens sat together. Crystal watching José… José staring into space. Renée's talk with Mr. Jensen had gone better than expected and the older man confessed genuine concern about separating the sisters and had agreed to reconsider. Renée hoped things would work out, because Crystal's crush on José was painfully obvious. Renée feared the longer the teens hung out together, the greater Crystal's chance of turning up pregnant.

Everyone peaceful for the moment, Renée allowed her mind to wander—to Duke. Always Duke. She'd met him less than a week ago, and already he took up more than his share of space in her head. First, she'd viewed him as nothing more than an annoying problem—a handsome, annoying problem. Tonight she'd witnessed a different side of the man—a vulnerable side that made her wish she wasn't going home alone later.

Her history with men was lackluster at best. The closest she'd come to a happily ever after had been her college sweetheart, Sean. They became engaged their senior year. Renée had been on top of the world until Sean's parents had paid her a visit on campus. His father was a well-respected surgeon and his mother a practicing psychologist. Both had expressed concern over Renée marrying their son.

They'd argued that Sean wouldn't have time for Renée when he entered medical school the following fall and that they hated to see her get hurt. Renée attempted to reassure them, claiming she'd be busy obtaining her master's degree in social work. When that didn't appease the couple, Sean's father spoke bluntly. Renée wasn't good enough for their son. Then they'd insulted her a second time by offering her money to break off her engagement to Sean. That day had been an eye-opener—Renée's first exposure to the way in which the rich controlled their world and those around them.

Was Duke any different from Sean's parents? He seemed to be a nice guy and his actions tonight proved that he cared about the plight of these kids. But was his concern because he had an agenda—to erect a new building on the property? If he didn't need to demolish the warehouse would he have been as generous with his wallet and his time?

When the train stopped at the Renaissance Center, Renée announced, "Wake up, everybody. We're here."

Clutching their souvenirs, the groggy kids stumbled off the train. Renée herded the group over to the statue of the *Siberian Ram* and conducted a head count. All present, she turned to lead the way to the visitor parking lot when Duke snagged her arm.

"May I speak with you privately?" Duke and Renée strolled out of hearing range, then he suggested, "Why don't the kids bunk down for the night in my hotel room. There's plenty of floor space. In the morning they can shower and eat breakfast before heading to—" he swallowed hard "—that damned warehouse."

Renée ached for Duke. He'd gotten in over his head with the kids and felt responsible for them. Dear God, she'd never meant for that to happen. She'd been in social work long enough that her heart had developed scar tissue thick enough to enable her to walk away when everything inside her rebelled. It had taken years of crying buckets of tears to accept that she'd never be able to help every child in need. Duke served as a reminder of how painful it was for outsiders to witness the children's suffering.

Shame filled her. She should have never agreed to this outing. "Duke—"

He held up a hand. "We can't allow them to sleep out in the cold one more night."

"Not *we,* Duke. Me. I'm the one responsible for the children."

"Let them sleep at the hotel, then tomorrow we'll locate a shelter that will accept all of them."

"They'll run from a shelter. They've done so before. Multiple times. That's why I've allowed them to remain in the warehouse."

"It's not right, Renée. Kids shouldn't have to live in cardboard boxes."

"Don't interfere, Duke. *Please.*" She walked off, leaving his protest stuck in his throat. After Renée and Duke retrieved their vehicles, the kids piled in and they drove to the warehouse.

With her trusty flashlight in hand, they navigated the stairwells to the top floor of the building. Save for Crystal who crawled inside the tunnel without a word of appreciation or even a goodbye, the rest of the kids were reluctant to end the evening.

"Thanks for taking us to the hockey game, Mr. D," Timmy said.

"Yeah, Mr. D, thanks for the bobblehead and stuff," Ricci and Willie both chimed in.

José snorted. "It's a stupid statue," he grumbled, clearly not ready to accept Duke's concern.

"And the pillow, too." Evie offered a sweet smile, then walked up to Duke and hugged his thigh.

The stark expression that crossed Duke's face caused Renée's throat to tighten with emotion.

"Can we go again sometime?" Ricci asked. The poor boy had no idea how expensive hockey tickets were.

"Time for bed," Renée cut in. "Everyone needs their sleep so they don't become ill."

Duke patted Evie's head, but the little girl balked at his leaving and clutched at his leg.

Renée pried the child's fingers loose and gave her a gentle push in the direction of the tunnel.

"Hey, Ms. Sweeney, we forgot to show you." Ricci scampered across the littered floor. "Point the light over here. We made a Christmas tree."

Renée directed the flashlight toward the far corner. Propped against the wall was a homemade Christmas tree made from bundled evergreen branches tied together with twine. The pathetic decoration made her eyes burn.

"It was Crystal's idea," Timmy explained.

Since the teen had already retreated for the night, Renée said, "Tell Crystal it's lovely."

"What do you think, Mr. D?" Willie asked. Everyone turned. "Where's Mr. D?"

Duke had vanished.

The kids rushed to the broken-out windows and stared at the parking lot below. Shoulders hunched, hands in his pockets, Duke strode toward his truck.

"He's mad at us." José swore.

"Mr. D is not angry," Renée said, then added, "He mentioned a cold coming on earlier this evening."

"You better go see if he's okay, Ms. Sweeney," Evie urged.

How like these kids to consider others before themselves. "Climb into the tunnel. I'll stop by tomorrow after work."

Once the kids obeyed, Renée hurried out of the building and across the parking lot. Duke sat in his truck, the engine running. When she stopped at the driver's side, he lowered the window.

"Everything okay?" she asked.

"No, Renée, everything is not okay. If you don't find those kids homes or get them to a shelter by first thing Monday morning, I'm going to the police."

Stunned, she watched Duke drive off, his threat hanging heavy in the air like the stench of decay and river water.

Chapter Six

"I'm glad you came to visit, Sam." Duke smiled at his stepsister, then focused on the road as he navigated his truck through Detroit traffic—nonexistent on a Sunday afternoon along the Riverfront.

"Me, too. I'm sorry for whining earlier in the week when we spoke on the phone, but Daddy's driving me nuts and I had to get away."

"Daddy's driving me nuts" was a familiar topic of conversation between the siblings. Dominick Cartwright was a natural-born controller.

"I miss Laura," Sam whispered. "Your mom always convinced Daddy to loosen his hold when he pulled the reins too tight around me."

"My mother spoiled you because she'd always wanted a girl and never had one of her own," Duke teased.

Sam wrinkled her nose. "Jealous?"

"Brat." In truth, Duke had been envious of the close relationship his mother had developed with her stepchildren. But Sam worshiped the ground Duke walked on, making it impossible for him not to fall under her spell, too.

"You probably invited me this weekend because you

felt sorry for me." Sam nibbled her fingernail. "But I don't care."

Actually he'd encouraged Sam to visit because he'd needed a distraction. Duke's gut was tied in knots and he blamed his sour mood on Renée and the kids camping out in his warehouse. After issuing the ultimatum Thursday, Duke had paced his hotel room until two in the morning. He hadn't been able to forget the stricken expression on Renée's face when he'd threatened to contact the police if she failed to remove the kids by Monday—tomorrow.

Since he'd discovered the kids' existence his conscience had been in a state of constant turmoil. One minute he worried about their safety, the next he attempted to forget they existed. Throw in a thousand thoughts about Renée…how he loved her cute dimples. How he dreamed of giving her a real kiss—long, hard and lots of tongue. How he yearned to hold her in his arms without heavy winter coats or bulky sweaters between them.

The situation wrecked havoc on his nervous system. In an attempt at self-preservation he'd asked his stepsister to fly up yesterday. Sam had been just the distraction he'd needed—until his head hit the pillow last night. Then his dreams had been hijacked by six faceless kids wandering the cold, dark streets, digging for food in garbage cans and crawling through cardboard-box tunnels that led to nowhere.

"Duke?" Sam poked his arm. "Earth to Duke…"

"Sorry," he muttered.

"You seem distracted."

No kidding. He had yet to figure out how one petite social worker and six street urchins had managed to upend his life. "I've got a lot on my mind." He turned on Atwater.

"Are you worried about the demolition delay?" Her brown eyes filled with concern.

Proceeding with the warehouse plans was the least of his worries. Renée and the kids had become his first priority. The problem was he liked Renée. *Really* liked her. Until he'd been thrust into Detroit's world of kids in crisis, Duke hadn't realized he possessed a soft spot for children. He had a feeling a relationship with Renée would always involve kids on one level or another and he wasn't sure he wanted to expose himself to the emotional upheaval she dealt with on a daily basis. Over time that kind of stress would take a toll on a relationship.

"Okay. You don't want to discuss business." Sam huffed. "Let's talk about Christmas." Her eyes flashed mischievously. "Holidays are meant to be spent with family."

Family. Maybe he had more in common with the kids he'd taken to the hockey game than he'd realized. At thirty-five he'd already lost both parents and his grandparents had been dead since his grade-school years, leaving him with only the Cartwrights—his stepfamily. *Only? You've got more family than the kids Renée's trying to help.* "I'll try to come home, but no promises."

"Good." Sam tossed her long black hair over her shoulder. "Did I thank you for taking me shopping?"

"Yes, you did," he grumped. Yesterday they'd driven through the Detroit-Windsor tunnel to shop in Ontario, Canada. For supper, he'd escorted Sam to the famous Penalty Box, home of the Chicken Delight. While they'd dined, he'd noticed how oblivious Sam had been to the stares of the men around them. Sam owed her exotic beauty to her Spanish ancestors on her mother's side. If not for the horse accident years ago, Sam would have probably been married by now.

After dinner, they'd made a pit stop at Casino

Windsor to gamble before heading back over the border. Today he'd promised a tour of the Riverfront before Sam left for the airport. "The warehouse is around the corner."

"This area needs a major facelift," Sam commented, her gaze surveying the buildings standing in various stages of abandonment and decay—blocks of overgrowth dotted with crumbling brick and stone. Not even the bright winter sun camouflaged the bleak despair that painted the area.

"Here we are." He pulled into the lot, staying at the far end, away from the broken-out windows on the fifth floor. He didn't want the kids spotting his truck.

"This is your new office?" Sam leaned as far forward as the seat belt allowed and stared out the windshield.

"Picture a modern glass-and-steel structure." He pointed toward the Detroit River to their right. "The top floors will consist of executive offices and condos with views of the river."

Sam continued to gape.

"What's wrong?" he asked.

"Are you positive you want to bring your company here?" She waved a hand. "Among all this desolation and poverty."

Call it pride or stupidity, but Duke intended for his company to grow and succeed in the Warehouse District. "This sounds crazy, but there's an emotion in the city that I've never experienced in any other metropolitan area. I can *feel* Detroit."

"Feel?"

"Rhythm is the soul of Detroit—cars, music, artists and sports. There are attractions for everyone here, if you search beyond the decay."

"That's very poetic."

He ignored her smirk. "People want to steer Detroit

back to its glory days when the cars rolled off the lines and Motown was king. I'll be a part of that by bringing my company's energy here."

Sam leaned across the seat and gave Duke a hug. "I'm proud of you for standing up to Daddy. One of these days I intend to do the same."

"What do you mean?" The declaration caught Duke by surprise. Sam's head injury had left her with a few lingering side effects like making snap decisions. Impulsive-something-disorder the doctors had labeled it.

"Once I figure out what I want to do with my life, you'll be the first to learn." She smiled. "I'm counting on you running interference with Daddy for me."

Great. Dominick Cartwright would accuse him of leading his daughter astray. He cast another glance at the fifth-floor widows.

Sam picked up on his preoccupation. "What are you staring at?"

Time to leave. "Nothing. We'd better head to the hotel." Five minutes later he pulled into the hotel visitor lot.

Once inside the room Duke scanned his e-mail while Sam packed her luggage. After a few minutes he shut down the laptop, then conducted a quick search of the suite to make sure Sam hadn't left anything behind. He spotted a pink bottle on the bathroom counter. "Hey, Sam, you forgot your perfume." He walked into the main room and froze.

"You have a visitor, Duke," his stepsister announced.

"Renée?" He'd intended to contact her after he'd driven Sam to the airport. He hoped Renée had stopped by to tell him she'd escorted the kids out of the warehouse.

"I'm sorry, I shouldn't have come." Renée's blue eyes traveled between Sam and Duke.

"I'm Samantha, Duke's stepsister."

Duke swore he heard a breath of air rush from Renée's lungs. Had Renée assumed Sam was his girl-friend or worse—a one-night stand?

"Renée Sweeney." The women exchanged handshakes.

"Sam's visiting from Tulsa." Duke glanced at his sister. "Renée's a social worker."

"C'mon in, Renée," Sam invited. "I'm packing for the airport." She continued to stuff shopping bags inside the luggage on the bed.

"I've caught you at a bad time," Renée apologized.

"Don't worry." He spoke quietly, hoping Sam wouldn't overhear.

"The Jensens have agreed to take both Crystal and Evie."

"That's great." The sisters wouldn't have to be sep-arated.

"Is he gonna come, Ms. Sweeney?" a child called from out in the hallway.

Duke poked his head around the doorjamb. Crystal and Evie waited by the elevator. He waved. "What's going on?"

"Evie refuses to go to the Jensens' unless you come along. She wants you to make sure it's safe for her there."

Renée expected him to deliver the girls to a foster home?

She does it all the time. And she does it alone.

His mind fumbled for an excuse. "Sam's flight leaves in a couple of hours and I've got to get her to the—"

"No, you don't, Duke," his stepsister interrupted.

He whirled and almost bumped Sam, who was eaves-dropping a foot away.

"I'll grab the hotel shuttle to the airport. You go and do…whatever." Sam smiled at Renée.

"Please don't change your plans," Renée begged. "I shouldn't have intruded."

Handing Duke his coat, Sam said, "I'll call you as soon as I land."

"Thanks for coming." Duke leaned in and kissed Sam's cheek.

With a wave, his stepsister shut the door in his face. He cringed at the notion of answering all of her questions the next time they spoke.

Renée refused to make eye contact as they walked to the elevator. The girls on the other hand…

"Mr. D!" Evie jumped into Duke's arms. He hugged her, noticing that she smelled like a little girl should—full of sunshine and sweetness. Her hair, freshly washed, sported a pink bow. Duke smiled at Crystal. Covered head to toe in black clothes, the teen had left off the dark eyeshadow, making her look younger.

"I hear you've got a new family." Duke straightened Evie's bow.

The child's skinny arms squeezed his neck. "I'm scared, Mr. D," she whispered.

"Everything will be fine, Evie. Let's go meet Mr. and Mrs. Jensen."

While they waited for the elevator, Crystal stared at the carpet, then as soon as the doors opened, she pleaded, "Promise you'll watch out for José."

Duke swallowed. He knew better than to make those kinds of promises, but he couldn't let Crystal down. "Sure. I'll keep an eye on him."

RENÉE QUESTIONED her sanity in inviting Duke along to the Jensens'. As they sat in the couple's living room getting acquainted, Renée reluctantly admitted she needed Duke's support as much as Evie proclaimed to.

Her boss's warning repeated in her head. "You can't afford to invest yourself personally in every child that comes along." Through the years, Renée had become attached to more children than she cared to confess, but the group living in Duke's building was special. The children had gotten to her in a way others hadn't. Maybe the fact that Christmas waited around the corner made her involvement more emotional. Whatever the reason, she'd better pull herself together.

"The junior high you'll be attending, Crystal, is within walking distance," Mrs. Jensen commented. "But Harry—" she nodded to her husband "—drives by the school on his way to the post office in the morning and he'd be happy to give you a lift."

Crystal ignored the older woman. Renée feared if the teen didn't drop the chip on her shoulder she'd ruin her and Evie's chances with the elderly couple. Mrs. Jensen retrieved a flyer from the table in the front foyer. "I picked this up from the school office." She handed the paper to Crystal. "Tryouts for the winter play are the week after Christmas break. And there are several after-school clubs if you're interested."

For the first time since entering the home, Renée noticed Crystal relax. "So it's okay if I join a club?"

"Of course. Harry can pick you up after he finishes his mail route."

Crystal's gaze roamed between the adults. "Don't I have to help with the other kids?"

Mr. Jensen cleared his throat. "This is how I believe we can make things work around here. Sundays after church, Crystal and Mrs. Jensen will prepare suppers for the upcoming week. The boys and I will clean the house."

"What about me?" Evie spoke.

Mrs. Jensen smiled. "You'll help with the cooking, of course."

"That way everyone gets to do the things they want to during the week," Mr. Jensen continued. "And the boss—" he winked at his wife "—will have time to rest during the day while you kids are in school."

"I like that plan." Crystal offered the older man a shy smile.

"Evie, I wonder if you might be interested in this." Mrs. Jensen handed a flyer to the child who hadn't left Duke's side since they arrived.

"What is it, Mr. D?" Evie held the paper an inch from Duke's nose.

"An invitation to join a Brownie troupe," he answered.

"What's a Brownie troupe?"

Renée came to Duke's rescue. "A Brownie is like a Girl Scout only for girls your age."

"Is Brownies fun?" Evie asked her sister.

"Probably," Crystal answered.

Evie slipped from Duke's lap and approached Mrs. Jensen's chair. "I get to be a Brownie if I stay with you?"

"If you want to, yes, Evie."

The child rested her tiny hand on Mrs. Jensen's knobby knee. "Would you be a Brownie with me?"

"Well, goodness, I haven't been a Brownie in years, Evie. But I believe I'd like to be one again."

The little girl smiled and Mrs. Jensen's eyes teared. At that moment Renée knew the Carter sisters would not only be safe and well cared for, but they'd thrive with the Jensens.

"Why don't you two come into the kitchen and help make a grocery list for our Christmas baking. We need to begin soon if we're going to bake enough cookies to give as gifts."

"You give your cookies away?" Evie asked in awe as she slipped her hand into Mrs. Jensen's and left the room without a word of goodbye to Renée or Duke. Offering an awkward wave, Crystal followed her sister.

Duke stood and fished his wallet from his pocket. He held out a wad of bills to Mr. Jensen. "I'd like to help with Christmas presents for the girls and the other children you're caring for."

"My wife and I will make sure Crystal and Evie have a present to open Christmas day."

"Evie wants Barbie Island Princess Rosella," Duke blurted, then smiled sheepishly at Renée. "She told me on the train." He switched his attention to Mr. Jensen. "Evie said Crystal enjoys fashion magazines and books. A fifty-dollar gift card to a local bookstore should work for her. If you or Mrs. Jensen don't have time to take Crystal to the bookstore, Renée or I will drive her there after the holidays."

Eyes burning, Renée pulled at a loose thread in her slacks. Duke had paid attention to Evie's ramblings on the train. Only a man who truly cared about a child would recall the name of a favorite Barbie doll.

Darn Duke Dalton for being…being…so *nice*.

"Use the rest of the money to take the family out for pizza or movies during the kids' break from school." Without another word, Duke dropped the cash onto the coffee table and walked out the front door.

"He's a generous man, Renée."

"That he is, Harry." She handed him her business card. She'd already given Crystal her number and encouraged the teen to call her if she needed anything. "I'll phone you in a few days to see how things are going." Once outside she hurried along the icy sidewalk. "Duke, wait!"

He paused by the truck door. "Thanks for coming with us today. The girls appreciated your support."

"How do you do this?" The misery in his gaze tugged at her heart.

"It's never easy." Then she squeezed his arm. "Crystal and Evie will be very happy with their presents Christmas morning."

"I'd hoped money would ease my guilt." Moist air streamed from his nostrils. "But no amount of money can make sense of having to find people to take in unwanted kids."

"In a perfect world, every child would have a family, but that's not reality. We do the best we can." Renée broached the subject she'd been dreading all weekend. "We need to discuss the others."

"Time's up, Renée. I want the boys out of the warehouse tonight." He hopped into the truck.

Panicking, she grabbed the door. "Are you hungry?" She was going to regret this. "I've got leftover chili and cornbread at home."

The starkness in his eyes lifted. "Chili sounds good."

"Follow me." She hopped into her car and drove to Church Street—less than two miles distance, but a world away from the Detroit Marriott.

She dreaded bringing Duke into her home—her private sanctuary. Once he walked out of her life, she'd be left with memories of him eating supper at her kitchen table. Yet, she acknowledged a curiosity about his family. She'd been stunned when another woman—a beautiful woman—had answered Duke's hotel door earlier in the afternoon. Even now she was confused and embarrassed over her relief at discovering Sam was Duke's stepsister.

Don't get involved with Duke.

Too late. She was in over her head and sinking faster by the minute.

Chapter Seven

The drive to Renée's took less than ten minutes. Darkness had fallen, but streetlamps and porch lights illuminated the area enough for Duke to read the historical marker claiming Corktown as Detroit's oldest surviving neighborhood dating back to the early 1800s. Victorian-era row houses restored to their former glory in vibrant hues and trimmed with gothic and Queen Anne details lined the street. Two inches of dingy, crusted snow blanketed the tiny front yards.

Duke's Realtor had given him a history lesson of the area when they'd toured Detroit. She claimed Irish immigrants had settled Corktown, but by the 1900s they'd scattered throughout Detroit's neighborhoods, leaving room for other newcomers—mainly people from the island of Malta. Duke had been impressed with Corktown's diversity, recalling a banner for the Maltese American Benevolent Society that hung between signs for Casey's Irish pub and The Works bar. A block west, flags of Mexico and Ireland had flapped above the Express bar. Corktown had been one of the few areas to avoid "white flight." With a mix of third- and fourth-generation residents and housing for a wide variety of incomes, the neighborhood had become a model for stable integration.

He trailed Renée's silver wagon for several blocks before turning right onto Church Street. She pulled into the driveway of a small mint-green cottage-style house with a detailed overhang and bay windows encased in fancy moldings. He parked on the street. The porch light illuminated the Christmas wreath that hung on the rust-colored front door. All the homes on the block sat on skinny lots with long driveways and no garages.

When Duke followed Renée into the house, he was immediately impressed by the detailed woodwork and stained-glass window in the entryway. "This is incredible." The ceiling moldings and baseboards had been restored and stained a rich mahogany color.

"Hang your coat here—" she motioned to an antique stand in the corner "—and make yourself at home while I warm up the chili." She walked through the narrow living room, which connected to a narrow dining room that led to the kitchen at the rear of the house.

He wandered about the living room, admiring the red-navy-and-gold rug that covered a good portion of the hardwood floor. Sturdy, traditional furniture filled the cozy space. A brick fireplace occupied the far wall and a big-screen TV sat on the floor at the end of the room. Evidently social workers made more money than he'd believed.

An image of him and Renée snuggled on the couch in front of a roaring fire watching a movie on the big-screen flashed through his head. Not a bad way to spend a winter evening in Detroit. He wandered over to the fireplace mantel to inspect the framed photos. A black-and-white wedding picture. A bust shot of a police cadet. And another photo of the man holding a baby with fuzzy blond hair—Renée?

Done nosing around, he strolled to the kitchen where he hovered in the doorway. Like the other rooms, this one had been renovated from top to bottom—stainless-steel appliances, oatmeal-colored tile countertops, which matched the floor tile and cabinets painted a distressed rusty-red. A rooster clock hung on the wall above the sink. "Your house is very nice."

The intimate smile she flashed triggered a tightening in his groin, catching him off guard. She was relaxed and at ease—maybe because they were on her turf. Duke fantasized that he'd get lucky tonight and steal a kiss from her.

"The house was built in the early 1900s," she said. "The floors and moldings are original, but restored. And the wiring had to be updated, as well as the plumbing and a hundred other things that cost a fortune."

"Who helped you with the work?"

"My brother and his partner. Pete's father is an electrician. They handled the electrical upgrades."

While Renée ladled chili into two bowls, covered the dishes with a paper towel and put them into the microwave, Duke studied her as he took a seat. He liked the way her blond hair swept across her cheek when she lowered her head and his hands twitched with the urge to run his fingers through the strands.

She set a plate of cornbread along with the butter dish on the table. Silverware, napkins and water glasses followed. Each time she passed him, he caught the scent of her shampoo. He closed his eyes and imagined spooning her in bed, sharing her pillow, burying his nose in her neck and drifting off to dreamland. The timer dinged, jarring him.

"Everything's ready." She delivered the steaming chili to the table.

He waited until she took her seat. She laughed. "What?" he demanded.

"Are you always so polite?"

"Most of the time." He made a show of placing his napkin in his lap. "This is excellent," he said after the first bite.

"People around here don't bother with *please* or *thank you*. It's implied." She buttered a piece of bread. "The neighborhood is one big family."

"Sounds like a nice way of saying everyone sticks their noses into your business." Duke couldn't imagine scrutinizing his neighbor's activities, nor did he care to.

"Unfortunately, yes."

"Did you make this from scratch?" He motioned to the cornbread.

"My mother did."

He glanced through the doorway wondering if the older woman was in the house.

"She lives next door," Renée answered his unspoken question.

The cornbread stuck in his throat when he swallowed, and he coughed into his napkin.

Renée let loose a belly laugh and Duke stared, mesmerized by the sound. He had a hunch she rarely laughed—social work didn't lend itself to humor.

"Call me crazy—" she sipped her water "—but I bought a house next door to my mother."

"I'd never choose to own a home near my mother if she were alive," Duke confessed. Residing one house away or a thousand miles wouldn't have cured his mother's habit of ignoring him.

"How did you lose your mother?"

"An ice storm hit Tulsa and she got caught in a

twenty-car pileup on the interstate. A semitruck hit her from behind." If his mother had remained home instead of attempting to drive into work, she'd be alive today. In the end death had been the one thing she hadn't been able to dismiss or ignore.

"I'm sorry, Duke." Renée squeezed his hand, her genuine sympathy reaching all the way to his heart. "Are you close to your father?" she asked.

"My dad died of cancer after I'd turned thirteen." Duke missed his father, but hoped his old man was proud of him.

"That must have been tough losing your dad at such a young age."

Tough? That was putting it mildly. Although his father had devoted long hours to his job, he'd attended Duke's baseball games and school activities whereas his mother had been too busy with her real estate career.

"My stepsister, Sam, has a brother named Matt. Their mother left them when they were toddlers and neither has seen her since." He cracked a smile. "The Cartwrights are my foster family."

Face sober, Renée set aside her spoon. "Since we're speaking frankly about families…" She took a deep breath. "I'm adopted, Duke. Rich's mother, Bernice, was my foster mother before she adopted me."

"I'd assumed you were a late-in-life baby, considering the age difference between you and Rich."

"You deserve an apology. I shouldn't have involved you in this mess with the kids. But I'd do it again if I had to. My goal is to find every child a loving home where they'll be nurtured by caring people just as I was."

Now Duke understood Renée's obsession with placing the kids in a home rather than a city shelter and her willingness to push the boundaries of the law to achieve that goal. He imagined she felt guilty that she'd been given a happy ending—adoption—while other children bounced from home to home or, worse, lived on the streets.

His admiration for Renée climbed another notch. She'd pursued a career that returned her to her roots. Such devotion convinced Duke that she'd always put the children first in her life. Even so, he wasn't ready to walk away from her.

"Your mother must be pretty special."

"My mother's seventy-nine, but I'll never be ready to lose her." Renée passed another piece of bread to Duke. "I work long hours and living close to Mom allows me to check in on her more often. And it's nice to arrive home to a meal waiting in my fridge."

"How old is your brother?"

"Fifty-four."

"And you're…?"

"Thirty-one."

"What happened to Bernice's husband?"

"He and his partner were shot and killed responding to a bank robbery."

"I imagine your mother worries about your brother." Duke's career in business had never given his mother a moment's concern—not that she'd have cared one way or another if he'd been a screwup at his job.

"Mom worries, but Rich has managed to remain safe all these years. He's one of the few officers in his precinct that hasn't been shot at."

Hero worship echoed in Renée's voice. The last thing Duke considered himself was a hero. When she slid her empty bowl aside, he said, "Time to discuss the boys."

Right then the kitchen door flew open and four police officers crowded into the room. Taken by surprise, Duke sprang from his chair, which crashed against the tile floor.

"Jeez, Rich. Ever hear of knocking? One of these days you might stumble in and find me in my nightie," Renée groused.

A snicker erupted from the rear of the pack. "You mean those flannel pj's you wear with the rabbit feet?"

"Shut up, Pete." With a heavy sigh, she waved a hand in front of her. "Duke, you remember meeting my annoying brother, Rich, and his wisecrack sidekick, Pete. The other two intruders are Jimmy and Tony. They're partners at the same precinct. Guys, meet Duke Dalton."

He shook hands with Renée's brother first, then the remaining officers.

Renée gathered the dirty dishes and carried them to the sink. "What do you guys want?"

The men stared at her in confusion, then Rich spoke. "The Lions are playing tonight."

"Shoot. I forgot." With a sigh of resignation, she said, "TV's all yours." Three of the cops sauntered out of the room. The one named Tony remained. "Any more chili left?" he asked with a hopeful grin.

Handing the officer a bowl, she said, "Help yourself."

While Tony heated the chili in the microwave, Renée washed dishes and Duke picked up the chair from the floor. His food hot, Tony left the kitchen.

"You're shell-shocked," Renée whispered, after the officer departed.

Before Duke figured out how to respond, the door opened again. This time an elderly woman carrying a large cake pan strolled in. Duke rushed forward to take the dessert.

"Thank you, young man." She smiled, her wrinkled cheeks red from cold.

"Mom. This is Duke Dalton. Duke, this is my mother, Bernice Sweeney."

"A pleasure to meet you, Mrs. Sweeney." Duke transferred the pan to the table, then offered his hand.

"The cake is for the boys." She covered her mouth and whispered, "My daughter's a lousy cook."

"I heard that, Mother."

Bernice ignored her daughter. "So you're the Okie?"

Renée had discussed him with her mother?

"Duke's new in town." Rich walked into the kitchen.

"If I remember correctly, Renée said you're moving your business from Tulsa to Detroit," Bernice commented.

"I bought a piece of property along the Riverfront that I plan to build on," Duke explained.

"That area sure needs a bit of cleaning up and—"

"Are you staying for the game, Mom?" Rich cut in.

"Oh, no, honey. I've got more knitting to do." She turned to Renée. "I'm using the new yarn you brought me the other day. I should have another afghan ready by the end of next week."

"Thanks, Mom." Renée hugged her mother.

"Nice meeting you, Duke." Bernice pointed a bony finger at Rich. "Don't you boys leave a mess in your sister's living room." She left and Renée followed.

"I'll call tomorrow, Mom." Renée remained on the porch, watching her mother make her way to her own home.

"Since you're from Tulsa, you must be a Cowboys' fan," Rich said to Duke.

"Actually, I cheer against the Cowboys."

Rich grinned. "The Lions scored. Why don't you watch the replay while I help Renée with the cake."

It wasn't an invitation—more like a command. With a lingering glance in Renée's direction, Duke left the room.

DRAT.

Sunday Night Football had derailed Renée's plans to discuss stalling the demolition. She shut the door and shivered. "Where's Duke?"

"Watching the game. How long have you two been dating?" Rich grabbed a stack of dessert plates from the cupboard.

"We're not dating," she protested. "We're—" *enemies* "—friends."

"Really?" He smirked.

"What's that goofy expression for?" Rich might be old enough to be her father, but that didn't give him license to lord it over her.

"Duke doesn't look at you like a *friend.*" Rich confiscated a steak knife from the silverware drawer and began cutting the cake.

No one, especially her brother, had to tell her that Duke was attracted to her. She'd been very aware of the way he'd studied her at the hockey game, the way his eyes watched her mouth when she spoke and how he had a habit of resting his hand at the small of her back when he opened doors for her. "Don't be ridiculous," she scoffed, hoping Rich would drop the subject.

He didn't. "I'm surprised you're speaking to the guy let alone dining with him."

Don't think I haven't questioned my own sanity.

Rich and her mother were aware of Renée's distrust of the wealthy. On numerous occasions her family had argued that not all rich people were the same. But one broken heart in a lifetime was enough for Renée. She had her reasons for keeping Duke at a distance—darned good ones if she said so herself.

Too bad Duke tested those beliefs daily. Rather than turn his nose up at her modest house he'd been impressed with the quality of the renovations. He hadn't minded eating at Mammy's—he'd even raved about the food. He hadn't become impatient when Willie had smeared ketchup on his coat at the hockey game, nor when Evie had rubbed her runny nose against his pant leg.

Renée wanted to believe Duke was being nice to the kids because he needed them evacuated from the warehouse. But a tiny voice in her head insisted that if Duke only cared about his interests he'd have reported Renée to the authorities days ago.

Duke was a good man and that was bad. *Very bad.* He truly worried over the fate of the children, which made her yearn to take a chance on him.

"Duke and I have very little in common," she mumbled, before asking her brother, "Need help with the cake?"

"Nice try." Rich grinned. "I kept my promise and haven't asked any questions about what you were doing in the Warehouse District a week ago Friday, but—"

"And I appreciate that," she said, intending to head him off. No such luck.

"Something's going on, Renée. I can feel it."

"That's your cop instinct going overboard."

"No, it's my big-brother intuition kicking in." He narrowed his eyes. "Are you breaking the law?"

She gasped, hoping she'd inserted the right amount of hurt to plant a seed of doubt in his mind.

"Don't get bent out of shape. I want to help."

"All I can tell you is that the less involved you become the better. I'm not going by-the-book on this one."

She glanced at the wall calendar. Christmas Eve was thirteen days away. She had to step up her efforts to locate homes for the boys—that is if Duke granted her more time.

"I've got connections. Favors I can call in," Rich offered.

Would it hurt to tell her brother the truth? "There are four runaways living in Duke's warehouse."

Instead of flipping out or losing his temper, Rich calmly asked, "How long have they been there?"

"I found them a couple of days before I—"

"Stood in front of the wrecking ball," he guessed.

"There were six, but I've placed the two girls in foster care. I'm working on finding homes for the four boys."

"You need to get them out. Yesterday they found a dead body in an empty lot not far from there. Slashed throat." He shoved his hands into his jean pockets. "I realize you hate the city shelters, but you don't have a choice. Better the kids take their chances there than run into a killer on the loose."

A cold chill wracked her body. "Any leads on the murderer?"

"Nope." He grunted. "I suppose you've kept your boss in the dark."

"I'm on probation, Rich. Not even being Detroit's Little Darling will save my neck this time if Harriet finds out."

"You've got twenty-four hours to get those kids out of there or I'll pick them up myself," Rich threatened.

"Fine." *Drat.* Now what was she going to do?

"I investigated him."

Him being Duke. Rich had developed a nasty habit of conducting background checks on her boyfriends— the few she'd had over the years.

"Dalton's clean," Rich chuckled. "Squeaky clean. His company deals with software technology, but then they all do these days. No complaints filed against his business. Pays his taxes on time. No bankruptcies. Phoned the Realtor who'd sold him the warehouse property and—"

"You're too much," Renée protested.

"No," he argued. "I'm too good. He's thirty-five. Never been married. No kids." He loaded the cake plates on the tray Renée had retrieved from beneath the sink. "His stepfather is in oil."

Curiosity got the best of her. "What kind of oil?"

Rich frowned. "What other kind is there? The stuff that makes people millionaires."

"His stepfather is a millionaire?" she whispered.

"Several times over. And over. And over."

And all along she'd believed Duke was well-to-do because he owned a successful business, not because he was related to a multimillionaire. "Well, it doesn't matter if his stepfather's rich enough to buy the entire state of Oklahoma. Duke isn't my type."

"Figured you'd say that." He scowled.

"People like Duke live in a world I want nothing to do with."

"Funny how that's the world you came from, isn't it?" Rich carried the tray of desserts into the living room.

Her brother's words hurt. She didn't appreciate being reminded of her lineage. Eyes stinging, Renée sucked in several deep breaths. Before she'd regained her composure, Duke wandered into the kitchen. "Rich mentioned you needed help with the dishes."

She handed him a towel. "You dry. I'll wash." After passing him a wet bowl she muttered, "Sorry about the intrusion tonight. I forgot about the football game."

"I wondered why you had a big-screen TV."

"That monstrosity was a housewarming gift from my brother. He needed an excuse to drop by without an invitation."

After a few more dishes were passed between them, Duke asked, "Have you ever dated any of your brother's cop friends?"

"A couple," she answered honestly. "But my job doesn't allow time for socializing." She turned off the water. "We need to talk."

"I'll stick around until the game is over."

Relief filled her with renewed energy, which she put to use scrubbing the sink. Shortly after ten, the guys filed out. Rich was the last to leave, his gaze cutting between Duke and Renée.

"I'll call you tomorrow," Renée told him. *And report in like I do with Mom.* Once the police cruisers had pulled away from the curb, she said, "My brother's—"

"Concerned. I'd be just as overprotective if I were him."

"About the boys." *Please God make Duke understand.* "I'm interviewing a couple on Wednesday who may take Ricci and Willie."

"What about José?"

"It's tougher to secure foster care for teens." She hated the thought, but… "José might end up in a facility for homeless young adults." Earlier in the week she'd called the Covenant House and had inquired on the availability of beds. Their Rights of Passage program allowed youths ages eighteen to twenty-two to live up to two years in the center while they attended school or vocational training. José didn't meet the age criteria, but the director had agreed to consider allowing him into the program on a temporary basis.

"And Timmy?"

"Timmy may end up in an orphanage for boys."

"Why an orphanage and not a foster home?"

"His physical handicap is an added responsibility most foster parents aren't willing to assume."

Jaw clenched, Duke insisted, "The boys shouldn't have to spend another night in the cold."

"You and my brother think alike." She sucked in a deep breath. "I've got twenty-four hours to make new arrangements for the kids or Rich is going to deliver them to a shelter."

"Why twenty-four hours? They should be picked up tonight." The stubborn angle of Duke's jaw revealed how strongly he felt about the boys' situation. If only she hadn't involved him… *No.* Without Duke the kids would not have experienced the hockey game and have the gift of that memory.

"Maybe I can convince the orphanage to accept all four boys." Willie turned seven in February. Surely they'd make an exception for the child and not separate him from the group. The orphanage would be better than a shelter, but not what she'd promised them—a real home.

"You do what you have to, but I'm not waiting any longer." Duke stalked out of the room and Renée hurried after him. "If anything happens to those kids I'll never forgive myself."

She lived with that feeling day in and day out—always second-guessing whether she'd sent the children to a safe home or if there were hidden dangers waiting for them behind closed doors. "Where are you going?" she asked when he grabbed his coat.

"To collect the boys."

Horrified, she demanded, "And do what with them?"

"They can bunk with me tonight."

"Are you crazy?" The guy was nuts.

"This way, they'll be out of the cold until you figure out what to do with them."

"Nice of you to offer, but if anyone discovers the children are staying with you, I'll lose my job." And wouldn't her boss love to bring the hammer down on Renée. When that didn't sway Duke, she added, "What about your reputation? People might jump to the wrong conclusion about you cohabitating with four boys in your hotel room."

"I don't care what people say."

Startled, Renée didn't immediately respond. Duke's unusual attitude surprised her. Most people cared a great deal about their good names and often their actions were a direct result of protecting their reputations.

"If you'd prefer, I'll sleep in an adjoining room and the boys will have the suite to themselves," he offered.

Right then, Renée swore she fell a tiny bit in love with Duke. "What will you do with four rambunctious boys?" Visions of pillow fights, wrestling matches and Willie piloting his body into the floor-to-ceiling windows flashed before her eyes.

"All I'll have to do is feed them and demonstrate how to operate the TV remote."

She rubbed the dull throb in the middle of her forehead. This wasn't right. And this wasn't Duke's problem. It was hers. "We'll bring the boys to my house. My mom will watch them while I'm at work."

"I'm not criticizing your mother, Renée, but the boys will take a toll on her."

"Mom will manage."

He snapped his fingers. "I've got it."

"Got what?"

"I'll stay at your house during the day and supervise the kids."

"You're offering to babysit?" Was he joking?

"As long as I have my laptop and cell phone I can do business anywhere."

Her first instinct was to say no. "Yes." Desperate times called for desperate measures. She prayed their plans wouldn't blow up in her face. "I leave for work at seven-thirty in the morning."

"Not a problem—" he flashed a sexy grin "—as long as you have a pot of coffee waiting for me."

"I can do coffee." But anything else was off-limits.

They were halfway to the warehouse when Renée received an emergency phone call to pick up a child whose parents had been taken to jail on charges of domestic battery.

"Problem?" Duke asked, pulling into the warehouse parking lot.

The situation was spiraling out of control. "How do you feel about sleepovers?"

Chapter Eight

"What do you mean, you quit?" Duke growled into his cell phone. He'd contacted Mr. Santori to give him the go-ahead to resume demolition of the warehouse. He hadn't expected Santori & Sons to walk off the job.

He paced Renée's tiny kitchen wearing nothing but boxers, not sure his body's sudden spike in temperature had to do with his anger or because the house was a damned sauna. "An unforeseen complication arose last week, but I give you my word there will be no more interruptions." Santori responded by putting Duke on hold to take another call.

Sweat beaded across Duke's forehead and he swiped at it. Last night after picking up the boys and their meager belongings, they'd stopped at Duke's hotel and he'd grabbed his laptop and a change of clothes before they'd headed to Renée's. Once they'd arrived at her house, she'd issued instructions for the boys to shower and go straight to bed, then she'd left to deal with the DCFS emergency.

While the kids took turns in the bathroom, Duke had gathered their dirty clothes and tossed them on the floor in the laundry room off the kitchen. Then he'd confiscated extra blankets from the linen closet and had made a large sleeping pallet on the living-room floor. Since there weren't enough blankets to go around, and the kids didn't have pajamas or clean clothes to change into, Duke had jacked up the heat, transforming the small house into the Amazon jungle. Once the four little Tarzans had drifted off to dreamland in their underwear, Duke had waited up for Renée.

When she hadn't arrived home by 1:00 a.m. he'd dozed off on the couch. He'd awoken at 3:00 a.m. Still no Renée, so he'd stripped to his boxers and stretched out on the couch under a sheet and had fallen asleep.

The smell of fresh-brewed coffee woke him at 7:00 a.m. He'd wandered into the kitchen, eager to see Renée, but found only a note taped to the microwave with her cell phone number scrawled on it. She'd come home, changed clothes and had left for another day of work.

"I'm here," Duke answered when Santori returned to the line.

The foreman was short and to the point. He'd taken another job and didn't have time to demolish Duke's warehouse. When Duke brought up the fact that Santori had signed a contract for his services, the man exploded, arguing that he hadn't dared decline the other job with Christmas around the corner and his men needing a paycheck.

By the time the foreman calmed, Duke had made up his mind to take his business elsewhere—even if it meant losing his deposit. He wanted the job done right and with Santori harboring ill feelings Duke didn't trust the foreman not to cut corners out of spite. With a disgruntled goodbye, Duke disconnected the call. "All because of a bunch of homeless kids."

"Did we get you in trouble, Mr. D?" Timmy hovered in the doorway, wearing a worried expression.

"No, Timmy. My argument with Mr. Santori had nothing to do with you or your friends," Duke lied.

The boy edged forward, dragging his twisted foot. He gazed up at Duke. "We weren't supposed to hide in your building, but I'm glad we did. 'Cause we met you and you took us to the hockey game." Timmy smiled. "That was the best night ever, Mr. D."

Heart swelling to football size in his chest, Duke ruffled the russet-colored hair. "You're right. That was the best night ever." At that moment Duke didn't care if he lost ten thousand dollars on the demolition project. Helping Timmy and the others was worth every cent.

The rooster clock read 7:30 a.m. "Why are you up so early?" Duke had expected the boys to snooze until noon.

Timmy shrugged. "I always get up early so I can get to the Dumpsters before anyone else does."

An image of Timmy Dumpster diving for food scraps made speech impossible. Duke opened the refrigerator and stared blindly at the contents. When was the last time his emotions had experienced such a workout? His mother's announcement they were moving to Oklahoma, he decided.

Feeling as if he needed to shore up his defenses to survive the day ahead, he closed the fridge door. "Breakfast might be awhile, Timmy. Why don't you watch cartoons and I'll call you when it's ready."

"Okay." The kid shuffled off, allowing Duke breathing room.

While he consumed his third cup of coffee, he rummaged through the cupboards, which were bare. He heard the TV turn on and assumed the other boys were awake. Duke scrambled a carton of eggs and toasted a half loaf of bread. Orange juice and milk rounded out the meal. After breakfast, he'd ask the kids to dress and tag along with him to the grocery store.

He borrowed three chairs from the dining room and called the group into the kitchen, where they squeezed together around the small table. No one complained about the meager fare.

"Aren't you gonna eat, Mr. D?" Ricci asked, jelly staining his cheeks.

There was barely enough food for the boys. Duke would survive on leaded coffee until lunch. He patted his belly. "I ate while I did the cooking."

Right then the door crashed open—someone needed to install a lock on the thing. In waltzed Renée's mother. Duke wasn't positive who was more shell-shocked— him, the boys or Bernice. In any event, everyone's mouth hung open.

Duke would have stood to greet Renée's mother, but feared she'd have a heart attack when she spotted his boxers. At the moment the older woman was having difficulty tearing her eyes from Duke's naked torso. "Renée forgot to tell you that she has guests staying with her, didn't she?"

Bernice shifted her gaze to his face. "Yes, she did."

"Boys, this is Ms. Sweeney's mother."

"You can call me Ms. Bernie."

"I'm Timmy." The boy pointed to his left. "He's Willie." The finger shifted. "That's José and Ricci." Then Timmy nodded at Duke. "And he's Mr. D. He and Ms. Sweeney rescued us from—"

"Whoa, tiger. Ms. Bernie just learned your names." Duke wasn't positive Renée wanted her mother to be privy to the details of the boys' situation.

"Is that all you're having for breakfast?" Bernice nodded at the table.

"As soon as we clean up the kitchen, we're heading to the grocery store."

"I hope you plan to wear more than your drawers in public."

Ricci giggled, then slapped a hand over his mouth when José shot him a glare.

"Yes, ma'am," Duke answered.

Bernice shrugged out of her coat. "Good Lord, it's hotter than hell's basement in here. Go on now. I'll take care of things while you dress." She went to the sink and began cleaning dishes.

"You heard Ms. Bernie. Hustle up, boys. And don't forget to brush your teeth."

"Awe, do we gotta brush our teeth?" Willie whined.

"Young man—" Bernice spun, then when she spotted the boys standing in their BVD's she whirled again "—Cleanliness is next to Godliness."

A chorus of "Huh?" filled the room.

"Besides," Bernice continued. "Girls can't stand boys with bad breath."

"Yeah, stupid." José nudged Ricci in the gut, then led the group from the kitchen.

Timmy trailed behind, grumbling, "But I don't want a girlfriend."

Duke stood, then froze when Bernice spoke. "I won't ask if there's anything going on between you and my daughter." She retrieved a clean dishrag from a drawer, sprayed glass cleaner on it, then polished the toaster. "But I'm warning you right now that if you break her heart, you'll answer to me." She glanced over her shoulder. "Is that clear?"

"Very." Duke considered reassuring Bernice that although he wouldn't mind exploring a more intimate relationship with her daughter, Renée was hesitant. But he held the words in, believing all Renée needed was time to admit her attraction to Duke.

"Do the boys have clean clothes to wear?" Bernice asked.

"Renée tossed in a load of laundry when she came home early this morning." Bernice frowned and he explained, "She answered an emergency call late last night. She was gone when I woke up."

"That girl works too hard," the older woman complained. "I'll toss the kids' clothes into the dryer. Then I'll make a casserole for supper. Renée will be too tired to cook."

"Has her job always been this demanding?" Duke asked.

"Yes. I wanted her to be a teacher. But she's felt a need to help the less fortunate. I guess because she feels blessed that her life turned out better than so many others who'd been dumped by their birth parents."

Renée had been abandoned? He'd thought maybe her mother had died in childbirth or had been a teenager who'd given her baby up. *Abandoned* sounded cold. Final. And very sad. He wanted to ask Bernice about the circumstances surrounding Renée's adoption, but chickened out.

Eyes twinkling, Bernice instructed, "You'd best put on your clothes before Mr. Morelli drops by and discovers I'm socializing with a naked man half my age. I spotted him a minute ago out walking his dog."

"I'll get dressed as soon as I fetch the paper off the front walk." Grinning, Duke left the room, Bernice's laughter ringing in his ears.

EXHAUSTED, RENÉE PARKED in her driveway, turned off the ignition and sat for a moment, staring at the front window of the house. Although the curtains had been drawn, miniature shadows danced about.

How had Duke's day gone? She'd been tempted to call him, but feared he'd demand she rescue him because he'd discovered how much work four rambunctious boys entailed. Oh, who was she kidding? Duke probably had everything under control. From the moment he'd arrived at the warehouse when she'd stood in front of the wrecking ball, she'd sensed he was a take-charge kind of guy—though she'd suspected the homeless children's situation had thrown him for a loop.

Tired as she was from lack of sleep, today had been a small success. Renée learned early in her career to appreciate the little victories as much as the larger ones. Wendy Altman, a retired schoolteacher, had agreed to take Willie and Ricci. Mrs. Altman had raised two sons of her own, while fostering children on and off through the years, but at sixty-two she was losing speed. Renée anticipated that the boys wouldn't have to remain with the widow more than a year before she placed them with a younger family.

A knock on the car window startled her. Her mother stood in the driveway holding a covered casserole dish. *Bless you, Mom.* Renée opened the door but *Hello* never made it past her lips before her mother hit the ground running.

"Imagine my surprise when I walked into your house this morning and found five half-naked males."

Renée smothered a smile behind her gloved hand. When she'd snuck out the backdoor earlier today, Duke had been covered from the waist down by a sheet, leaving his bare chest—hairless, muscular and just the right amount of *Ahh*—exposed for her perusal.

"They were eating breakfast in their underwear, daughter. What will the neighbors say?"

"They didn't parade around the block in their Skivvies, did they?"

Her mother's mouth twitched. "Only the big boy…he went outside to grab the morning paper."

Oh, Lord.

"I realize I've been pestering you to marry and give me grandchildren, but aren't you rushing things with this Duke?"

A gust of wind shoved Renée against the car door. It was freezing outside and the casserole would be cold by the time they got in the house. "It's not like that between me and Duke."

"Then someone needs to tell that poor man."

"What?" Her mother wasn't making sense.

"I noticed the way he stared at you last night when I brought the cake over. The man is smitten."

First Rich. Now her mother.

"Mom, you're used to being around rough-talking cops so it's natural you mistook Duke's good manners for *smitten.*"

"If you refuse to discuss the man, then we'll talk about the children. Is your boss aware that you're harboring runaways in your home?"

Her mother was far too perceptive for a woman of advanced age. "Mum's the word."

"And if the neighbors ask questions?"

"They're relatives visiting for the holidays."

"Renée dear." Her mother sighed. "Two of the boys are Hispanic and one is black."

"So they're adopted family members."

"And what do you expect me to tell them about Duke—that he's adopted also?"

The conversation was going nowhere and Renée's numb toes tingled. She extracted the dish from her mother's grasp and they marched up the driveway to the rear of the house.

"He took the boys grocery shopping today."

Guilt pricked Renée. Duke was too generous with his wallet. Then again maybe she shouldn't feel bad that the stepson of a multimillionaire paid for a few groceries.

"I brought over extra pillows and blankets. And that ridiculous blow-up mattress Rich gave me for Christmas years ago. I never have figured out what I'm supposed to do with that thing."

Renée believed her brother had given the mattress as a gift so that if he broke up with a girlfriend he'd always have a bed at his mother's house.

They paused at the bottom porch step. "Your Duke's a nice man."

"He's not *my* Duke, Mom." The protest sounded feeble to Renée's ears.

"You could do worse than a gentleman, dear."

"No matchmaking schemes, Mom. Duke and I are working together to help the boys. Once they're settled in homes, he'll go his way and I'll go mine." Besides, even though the man was genuinely nice…and handsome…and smelled good…and had a sexy smile… she'd never be accepted by his world. She didn't have the proper pedigree.

A thoughtful gleam filled her mother's eyes. "One of these days you're going to have to let go of the anger and resentment. Until you do, you'll never be at peace."

The blunt words tore at Renée. All she'd ever wished was to make Bernice proud, so the woman would never regret raising her. But letting go wasn't as easy as her mother believed. Not many people had experienced the kind of betrayal Renée had.

"You need to get those boys situated soon. Mr.

Morelli put out a block alert, informing the neighbors that a strange man and a bunch of hooligans have moved in with you."

"Maybe if you'd go out on a date with him, he'd stop the Scrooge routine." Renée climbed the porch steps, then paused at the top. "Aren't you coming?"

"Too much racket for my old ears."

Renée cracked the door and bursts of raucous laughter escaped. What in the world was going on in there? "Thanks for supper, Mom."

"Make sure you eat, too. And sleep. You look terrible." After delivering the parting shot her mother cut through the gap in the hedge between their properties and entered her own home.

When Renée stepped into the kitchen, shouts, tires squealing and high-powered car engines threatened to deafen her. She rested the casserole dish on the stove, then laid her coat, scarf and gloves over a kitchen chair. The warm temperature inside the house caused her nose to run and she grabbed a tissue from the box on the counter.

"How was your day?" Duke lounged in the doorway wearing jeans and a T-shirt. No shoes or socks. Barefoot, gorgeous and sexy. The first words that rushed into her head—*I missed you.*

"Quieter than yours," she shouted.

His half grin sent her stomach into a flip. Shoving away from the doorjamb, he admitted, "I'm not very good at saying no."

"They ran roughshod over you?"

"Yep." His sheepish wince made her laugh. The big bad corporate cowboy had been defeated by a bunch of miniature monsters.

"What's with the noise?" she asked.

"I bought an Xbox system and hooked it up to the big screen. They're playing a NASCAR game."

If he'd stop doing nice things she might stand a chance at remaining immune to him. "You're spoiling them, Duke."

Ignoring her censure, he lifted the foil on the casserole dish and sniffed, then grimaced. "What's this?"

"Tuna fish and noodles."

Eyes pleading, he suggested, "How about Chinese?"

"You don't care for tuna fish?"

"Not really."

"Besides the boys harassing you all day, anything else happen?"

"Mr. Santori walked off the job."

More guilt. If she'd taken the kids from the warehouse earlier, Duke's business plans wouldn't have been interrupted. "I'm sorry. Would it help if I spoke to the man?"

Duke chuckled. "The moment he spotted you, he'd run in the opposite direction."

"Ha, ha." All things considered, Duke appeared to be taking this latest roadblock in stride. A tiny crack ruptured in the wall around her heart and before Renée realized her actions, she rose on tiptoe and pressed a soft kiss to Duke's whiskered cheek. She meant to offer comfort, but as soon as her lips touched his skin, she caught a whiff of faded aftershave and she was lost.

When he turned his head, she didn't protest the meeting of their mouths. His lips brushed over hers with ease, guiding their kiss in a more erotic direction. His hand found her hip, his fingers tracing the bone before drifting subtly over the curve of her bottom. His other hand snuck beneath her hair, fingers pressing against her scalp, holding her head steady while he deepened the kiss.

His tongue traced her bottom lip and she moaned,

her body melting. She opened her mouth to his searching tongue and entwined her arms around his neck, pressing her breasts to his chest. His scent, his hardness, his *everything* overwhelmed her and she gladly lost herself in Duke.

"Yuck!"

Renée felt Duke stiffen, but she kept her eyes closed and her mouth on his.

"Hey! Mr. D's kissing Ms. Sweeney."

Duke broke off the kiss and faced Ricci who flashed a goofy smile. The other three boys joined their friend in the kitchen. "You guys gonna get married?" Willie asked.

Ignoring the pip-squeak's question, Renée said, "Wash up. Suppertime." Two minutes later the boys were seated at the table and Renée filled their plates with casserole. Duke poured four glasses of milk, then excused himself to monitor his e-mail and retreated to the dining room.

Renée half listened to the boys' chatter, adding comments when appropriate, but her mind remained on Duke. Why had she allowed him to kiss her? Did it mean anything to him? Did she want it to mean anything to him?

"I heard you went grocery shopping today. What did you buy for meals?" she asked the group during a lull in conversation.

The boys exchanged puzzled glances.

"We didn't pick up any supper foods." Duke confessed from the doorway, his expression contrite.

Renée went to the fridge and stared at the contents. Next, she opened the freezer, then the pantry and the cupboards. "There's nothing here but junk food."

"We went a little overboard—"

"A little?" she interrupted Duke. "I hope you own stock in Hostess."

"Can we have Twinkies for dessert?" Willie asked.

Just what a hyperactive boy needed—more sugar. "Maybe," Renée answered. "Finish your supper."

Less than five minutes later, the group left the table and resumed playing the video game in the living room. "Still interested in Chinese food?" Duke asked.

Renée was tired enough to hit the sack. But the hope in Duke's eyes lent her renewed energy. "Sure. Mind if I take a bath and hop into my pajamas while we're waiting for the food?"

"Go ahead." He snagged the phone book off the counter. "I'll call in our order."

"Here." She handed him a coupon from her favorite Chinese take-out restaurant. "I like everything on the menu and they deliver," she announced, then left the room.

Duke anticipated the cozy dinner with adult conversation…and hopefully another kiss from Renée—traces of her taste clung to his lips. He'd thought of her all day. Wondered where she was. What she was doing—a first since his breakup with Elizabeth.

Once he'd ended his relationship with the lawyer in Tulsa, he'd settled into a pattern of casual dating. Since his arrival in Detroit he hadn't had the time or the interest in dating—until Renée and the homeless munchkins landed in his life.

After ordering a variety of food, he put a movie in for the boys and flipped off the living-room light. A half hour later when the food arrived, Renée had yet to leave the bathroom. He waited another fifteen minutes, then knocked on the door. "Everything okay in there?" No answer. He knocked louder. No answer.

Had she fallen asleep? Or worse, slipped under the water and…? He felt along the door molding until his fingers bumped into a stick key. He popped the lock, then opened the door a crack and poked his head in.

Wrapped in a fluffy pink towel, Renée stroked a razor up her shaving-cream covered calf, her cute fanny swaying to the music playing on her iPod headphones.

She must have sensed his presence, because she glanced over her shoulder, then squawked and yanked her headphones from her ears. "What are you doing?" Her breathless question incited a bathroom fantasy inside Duke's head. He and Renée in the tub, up to their chins in bubbles, their slick bodies rubbing together…

"Duke?"

"Sorry. Food's here." He shut the door and retreated to the kitchen to cool off. A few minutes later, Renée joined him, wearing a pink robe, bunny slippers and smelling of floral-scented lotion. She stared at the take-out containers on the table and nibbled her lower lip.

Ah, damn. She regretted their kiss. "What's wrong?"

"If I ask you a question will you tell me the truth?"

He had nothing to hide. "Sure."

"How much money did you lose to Mr. Santori?"

Relieved that her concern had nothing to do with him kissing her, Duke answered honestly. "Three thousand."

She sank into a chair at the table. "This is my fault."

"No," Duke protested, even though his subconscious disagreed. "Santori's a schmuck." Duke had hated losing the deposit. But he hated more that Renée fretted over the situation. She had enough worries of her own without taking on his.

"What will you do?" she asked.

"Wait until after the first of the year to move forward with the plans for the warehouse." He'd spoken to the companies he'd gotten bids from previously, but all were tied up with jobs for the next few weeks.

Renée said nothing for a long time, her bunny slipper bobbing up and down. Finally she whispered, "Do you plan to spend time with your family in Tulsa while you wait for the demolition to resume?"

"That depends."

Her blue eyes blinked. "On...?"

"On whether you want me to stay or leave."

Her tongue snuck out and licked her lower lip.

C'mon, Renée. Take a chance on us.

"I want you to stay."

Yes! "I was hoping you'd say that."

Chapter Nine

Another day confined in Renée's house and Duke would lose his mind. "Hey, guys," he called from his seat at the kitchen table. No answer. Not that he expected to be heard over the roar of NASCAR exploding from the TV speakers.

He closed his laptop. After responding to e-mails he'd phoned his manager in Tulsa and discussed a personnel issue. Then he'd RSVP'd for a meeting that had been scheduled for January 4 with the community development board he'd been invited to serve on when he'd accepted Detroit's incentive package to relocate his business to the Warehouse District. Duke had yet to become involved in any issues the board was dealing with, but one member had informed him that they would address a second proposal for a recreation facility. The board had rejected the plans before Thanksgiving, but this particular person was a thorn in the board's side and refused to accept defeat.

Business taken care of he considered returning his stepsister's calls, but wasn't in the mood to field questions about his relationship with Renée—as if he had a clue where they stood. The previous evening after he and Renée had eaten Chinese takeout, he'd said goodbye. Later that night he'd stretched out on the king-size bed in his hotel room and replayed their kiss over and over in his mind, picking apart every detail.

Her breath soughing across his lips.

The tips of her fingernails pressing into his biceps.

The nudge of her nose against his cheek.

The clean smell of her skin and hair.

The taste of her mouth—heady and sweet like a shot of Amaretto.

She wouldn't have asked him to remain in Detroit for the holidays if the kiss hadn't meant *something* to her. He was physically attracted to Renée, but he also admired who she was and what she did each day to help children. Yet he worried that what he admired most would get in the way of a relationship with her.

For years Duke believed he'd worked long grueling hours, but his day at the office was nothing compared to Renée's. She put in more than eight hours, as well as Saturdays and Sundays on occasion. He understood kids in crisis didn't vanish at 5:00 p.m., but he refused to settle for the number two spot in Renée's life.

Would the little time she carved out for them be enough to really get to know one another—and he wasn't referring to learning her favorite color or the kind of movies she enjoyed watching. Nor did he mean family—he'd already met her brother and mother. They were likable, caring, down-to-earth people. What bothered him was that he couldn't shake the feeling Renée was keeping a secret about her past. Who had made her wary of the wealthy? One thing for sure, he wouldn't find the answer staring at the kitchen walls. He carried his coffee mug to the sink.

"Hey, guys," he shouted.

José paused the game. The teen rarely spoke, but acted more relaxed around Duke than he had at the warehouse.

"What do you say we get out of here and go Christmas shopping," Duke suggested.

Ricci and José exchanged frowns, then Ricci said, "We don't have any money."

"Let me worry about the money." Duke had given himself and his employees a holiday bonus. He'd intended to use the money to furnish his condo in the new building. For the past couple of weeks he'd slowly chipped away at the sum. He figured if the kids had to live in cardboard boxes, then his old furniture would suit a while longer.

Timmy put aside the game controller and stood. "Who should we buy presents for?"

"Ms. Sweeney. And Crystal and Evie." Surely giving the girls a few gifts wouldn't break any rules.

"That would be cool," José finally spoke—probably because their errand had to do with Crystal. Duke assumed the teen missed the girl.

Ten minutes later they piled into the truck. When he drove off, he noticed the curtain flutter in Bernice's front window. Renée had probably instructed her mother to spy on him and the boys. He considered inviting the older woman along, then nixed the idea. He intended to buy Renée a gift and didn't want Bernice's opinion on the purchase. While the kids argued over video game strategies, Duke drove to the Millender Center across the street from his hotel. Once they entered the shopping mall they made a pit stop for lunch at the food court.

With their stomachs full, they began shopping. Timmy purchased a bag of chocolate snowmen for Renée from BonBons Candy & Godiva Chocolatier. Then he added treats for the girls and Bernice. Ricci wanted to buy Renée a Santa bear from the Hallmark store and all the boys agreed that Evie would like the pink princess teddy bear. Willie broke a snow globe flying his plane through the aisles and Duke ended up paying for that, as well. At least the boy felt bad enough about the incident that he behaved. After those purchases, the kids decided Renée needed a Red Wings baseball cap to go with the jersey Duke had given her. José selected a black scarf with silver skulls sewn into it for Crystal.

After round one of shopping, Duke treated the gang to soft pretzels and drinks, then asked them to wait outside the jewelry store while he browsed. He figured he had fifteen minutes max before Willie's airplane took off again and landed somewhere it shouldn't.

"I'd like to see your diamond earrings," Duke said to the salesclerk.

The man's face brightened. "Right this way, sir." He placed a tray of jewelry on the counter, the earrings ranging from two hundred to one thousand dollars.

Duke envisioned Renée's blond hair. "Do you have emeralds?" When the clerk presented a second tray of items, Duke frowned. The jewelry looked…cheap.

"Perhaps a nicer piece," the clerk suggested, presenting a smaller sampling of earrings.

Much better. Duke indicated the emerald teardrop earrings and a matching teardrop necklace. They were perfect for Renée.

She'll hate them.

But they're beautiful and the quality is acceptable, he argued with his conscience.

She'll insist the money you spent would have fed and clothed a hundred needy kids.

He handed the earrings to the salesclerk. Renée would probably hock the pieces and use the money for a worthy cause. He wanted to give her a trinket that said...*I'm falling for you.*

Pearls.

Why hadn't he considered them before? His father had given his mother a pearl necklace on their wedding day. When his mother had become engaged to Dominick, she'd tossed the pearls onto Duke's bed, confessing that she'd never cared for the piece of jewelry. She'd given Duke her permission to pawn the strand. From that day forward Duke questioned whether his mother had ever really loved his father.

"I believe I'll pass right now."

Obviously disappointed, the salesclerk muttered, "As you wish, sir." He whisked the box from the counter. Duke sauntered over to the bench outside the store where he'd instructed the boys to sit.

"What did you get Ms. Sweeney, Mr. D?" Ricci asked.

"Nothing yet." Duke noticed Timmy staring into space. "Not feeling too well, buddy?" Duke pressed his hand against the boy's flushed cheek. His skin was on fire. "Upset stomach?" He shouldn't have bought the snacks so soon after lunch. Timmy stared at Duke with glassy eyes. Worried that the kid might have contracted more than a cold, he announced, "Time to head home."

Duke led the way to the escalators. Before they stepped on, he swooped Timmy into his arms. He expected a protest—instead, the kid rested his head against Duke's shoulder and closed his eyes. Duke's lungs squeezed with panic. If he'd stayed in the house like Renée had asked...

When he pulled up to Renée's, he ordered Timmy to remain in the truck, while he let the others into the house. He told the boys to put in a movie and behave, then he went next door and asked Bernice to watch the kids while he took Timmy to a doctor. Bernice gave Duke her physician's name, phone number and directions to the health clinic, then offered to call ahead and alert the staff that they were on the way.

As soon as Duke and Timmy arrived, a nurse escorted them to an exam room, stopping to weigh Timmy at the scale.

"Fifty-four pounds." The nurse scrawled on the chart.

Wasn't that underweight for a boy his age? The nurse must have read Duke's mind. "Timmy needs to gain a few pounds. Are you eating lots of Christmas cookies?"

Too exhausted to answer, the boy leaned his head against Duke's arm for support.

Once in the exam room, Duke hoisted Timmy onto the table. The nurse took his temperature and blood pressure. "Dr. Morgan will be in shortly." She handed Duke a clipboard of paperwork, before leaving.

"The doc will fix you up in no time, Timmy. I promise." After scanning the forms Duke asked, "When's your birthday?"

"August 10."

"You're how old again?"

"Nine."

Duke left several questions unanswered—mother's name, father's name, address and telephone number. When the nurse popped in again, he advised her that he intended to pay for the visit with a credit card and wouldn't be filing an insurance claim.

"We'll worry about that later. Dr. Morgan will be right in."

In less than five minutes a short man with a Santa Claus beard and belly to match waltzed through the door. "I hear you're not feeling too well, Timmy."

The boy offered a weak smile.

Duke shook hands with the doctor. "Duke Dalton. Bernice Sweeney recommended your clinic."

"I see quite a few of Renée's kids." He coaxed Timmy into a sitting position, then listened to the boy's lungs. "I suspect pneumonia, but we'll take an X-ray to be sure." He peeked in the boy's ears, nose and throat, then felt the lymph nodes around his neck. "After the X-ray, Timmy needs fluids. He's dehydrated."

The nurse whisked Timmy from the room, leaving Duke to wait alone. He contemplated phoning Renée, but figured Bernice had already updated her on the situation. Besides, he wasn't in the mood for a lecture. He understood that Renée feared if he took the boys out in public he might run into her coworkers or her boss and risk them discovering she hadn't followed department protocol. But something had to give. The kids were going stir-crazy in her house.

The nurse returned with Timmy, then proceeded to start an IV. After a few minutes, the boy fell asleep. Duke sat next to the exam table, fearing if he left, Timmy might roll off and smack his head against the floor. Duke monitored the rise and fall of the boy's skinny chest, his throat swelling uncomfortably at the knowledge that this child was alone in the world.

His cell phone went off inside his coat pocket and Duke scrambled to answer it before the noise woke Timmy. "Hello," he whispered.

"You haven't answered my calls."

Damn. He should have glanced at the caller ID. "Hey, Sam."

"Why are you whispering?"

"I'm in a doctor's office with one of Renée's kids."

"Your girlfriend has children?"

"Renée's a social worker, remember?"

"Oh, that's right."

"She's trying to locate homes for a group of kids that were living in the warehouse."

"Your warehouse?"

"Yeah. That's why I had to put the demolition on hold."

"What happened to the kid you're with now? Did he get hurt?"

"The doctor believes Timmy has pneumonia."

"Where are the others?"

"Renée found a foster home for the two girls. No luck yet for the boys."

"Are they runaways?"

"Yep. Living off the streets."

"I can't imagine," Sam murmured.

That was the truth. His stepsister had grown up wanting for nothing.

"So the boys are staying in your hotel room with you?" she asked.

"No, they're living at Renée's and I'm watching them during the day."

Sam paused. Duke could practically hear her mind processing what he'd said. "That's generous of you. You must really care for this woman."

Why deny it? "Renée is special." Then he asked. "What's up with you?"

"I wanted to tell you that Matt won his event at the Dodge National Circuit Finals Rodeo in Pocatello."

"That's great. I'll give him a call later to congratulate him."

"Better yet, fly home for Christmas and congratulate him in person. And bring Renée."

"There's no guarantee these kids will be in foster homes by then."

"Then bring the kids with you. Daddy will send his private jet."

What would the oil king think of Renée's Detroit family tree—then again he didn't give a crap whether his stepfather approved or not. "I'll discuss it with Renée and get back with you," he promised. The exam-room door opened. "Gotta go." He disconnected the call.

While the nurse unhooked Timmy's IV, she confirmed the doctor's diagnosis of pneumonia and administered Timmy's first dose of an antibiotic. The nurse said the doctor had phoned in a prescription at a pharmacy and Renée would pick it up on her way home from work.

He carried Timmy to the waiting room and set him in a chair, then fished his wallet from his pocket and approached the registration desk. When he offered his credit card, the nurse waved him off with a smile.

"Everything's taken care of."

Duke appreciated the doctor's generosity and questioned how many times he'd helped Renée's kids without accepting payment for his services. Duke left a hundred-dollar bill on the counter and walked away.

"Time to go home, kid." He carried Timmy to the truck, then navigated the dark neighborhood streets. He glanced at his sleeping passenger curled up on the front seat and rested a protective hand on the boy's shoulder.

This was certainly turning into a Christmas to remember.

"How's he doing?" Rumpled and worried, Duke stood outside Renée's bedroom wearing a T-shirt and boxers.

She'd asked Duke to sleep on her couch in case she had to rush off in the middle of the night on a DCFS emergency. She didn't dare leave a sick child alone.

Sympathy for Duke tugged at her. He blamed himself for the boy's illness.

"Right now my star boarder is grumpy," she muttered, gently tugging the child into a sitting position on the blow-up mattress next to her bed. "He doesn't want to take his medicine." At half past two in the morning the other boys were fast asleep on the living-room floor. She'd assumed Duke had been in dreamland, too, but he must have heard her rummaging around in the kitchen.

After Timmy finished his medicine and milk, she tucked him under the covers. He was asleep before she turned out the light. Duke followed her to the kitchen and stood in her shadow while she rinsed the glass. "Stop hovering," she scolded with a smile. He hadn't let her or Timmy out of his sight all night.

"You're angry with me, aren't you?" He tunneled his fingers through his hair.

Yes, she was annoyed that Duke had taken the kids Christmas shopping—but only because he was spending too much money on them. "Can we talk about this tomorrow?" She was dead tired. Stress had a way of tiring a person even if they sat at a desk all day talking on the phone.

Before she'd taken two steps, he'd grabbed her arm. His brown eyes flashed. "I can't fix whatever's wrong unless you tell me what it is."

A faint whisper of aftershave mixed with Duke's unique male scent tickled her nose, sidetracking her thoughts for a moment. She stepped out of smelling range. *Better.* "You assume there's a solution or a reasonable explanation for everything, don't you?" And why wouldn't he? His world made perfect sense. Hers never did.

"What do you mean?"

"Since the moment we met you've wielded your wallet like a sword."

"What does that have to do with you being angry at me for leaving the house with the kids?"

Nothing—except each time he opened his billfold she was reminded of how frustrating her world was because of a lack of money. She worked her butt off, assisting kids in need and fighting obstacles she didn't have the means to get around.

"Sorry I snapped," she apologized, hating herself for being jealous of Duke's generosity.

As he tucked a strand of hair behind her ear, his finger stroked against her skin, making her shiver. "You're overworked. You need a vacation." He grinned. "Somewhere warm like the Bahamas."

She rolled her eyes. "Very funny."

"You have purple smudges beneath your eyes." His finger drifted from her ear to her cheek.

"Flattery will get you everywhere." She should walk away. And she would, but first… She turned her head. His finger inched closer to her mouth. Her eyelids grew heavy.

Then… His mouth pressed against hers. Soothing… cajoling.

"I want to make love to you," he whispered.

The words startled Renée, and she slipped from his hold.

"Don't you—"

"No." Actually, sex with Duke would be incredible. The problem lay in preventing her heart from turning the physical exercise into a lovemaking experience, which would inevitably leave her shattered.

"I guess I misjudged your feelings." Duke dropped his gaze to his bare feet.

She caught his fingers in hers, this time stopping *him* from walking away. "You didn't misjudge anything." She waited until he made eye contact. "I like you." After a deep breath, she conceded, "A lot."

The relief in his gaze was painful. "I'm glad."

"But nothing's going to happen between us."

His jaw sagged.

"We're too different," she argued. "You and I were thrown together by circumstance. If not for our desire to help these kids, our paths would never have crossed."

"Once the boys are in homes, you and I will have more time to—"

"About the kids," she interrupted, not wanting Duke to get his hopes up. "Tomorrow I need to take Ricci and Willie to meet Mrs. Altman."

"What about José?"

"Mrs. Altman doesn't feel she can handle a teenager."

"José's a good kid. If she met him—"

"I appreciate you defending José, but I can't force him on an old woman or she'll refuse all the boys."

"Where will José go?"

"I've secured a bed for him at the Covenant House."

"What's that?"

"An outreach program for homeless young adults." In Renée's opinion, the staff at the Covenant House was top-notch. Each youth received counseling, as well as an assigned mentor.

"José's not a young adult," Duke objected.

"They're making an exception. In the meantime I'll continue to work on lining up a foster home for him."

"When does José leave?"

"After Ricci and Willie are dropped off at Mrs. Altman's."

"And Timmy?"

"He's on a waiting list for a bed at the Edwin Danby Memorial Children's Home." An orphanage for boys.

"It doesn't seem fair."

Although she was secretly glad Duke had assisted her with the kids, the misery in his eyes broke Renée's heart. No matter how many times she delivered a child to a foster home, shelter or orphanage she felt as if she was abandoning them rather than helping to improve their situation. "Life isn't fair. These kids have learned that lesson earlier than most. Some days I find that hard to take."

"But you do so much for children, Renée."

"And it's never enough." She shook her head. "Even after I've placed a child in a home there's no guarantee they'll receive the nurturing guidance they deserve and need to grow into productive adults." No assurance they'll receive praise, encouragement or even a hug from their foster parent.

"What about you?" he whispered, curling his hand around her neck. "Who nurtures you every day?" He tugged her against him, wrapping his arms around her waist. She burrowed her nose in his T-shirt and struggled against the urge to allow Duke to slay her dragons.

After a long hug, he said, "C'mon. I'll tuck you in for the night." He walked her to the bedroom, held the covers up while she slipped into bed, then kissed her cheek. "Sweet dreams, angel," he whispered from the doorway.

Why Duke? How had she fallen for a wealthy man when experience told her that money and status drove people to commit heartless acts?

Duke isn't merciless. He's proven that he's a good guy. Give him a chance.

Did she dare?

Chapter Ten

"Cool!" Crystal exclaimed when she opened the gift the boys had purchased for her. She wrapped the black scarf around her neck and struck a pose that made everyone laugh. Her eyes connected with José's and Duke smothered a grin at the red hue that darkened the teen's cheeks. The young man definitely had a crush on Crystal.

Stomach full from the holiday dinner Renée's mother had prepared for the group, Duke took in the scene unfolding before him in Bernice's living room. Renée snapped pictures, while wrapping paper flew in all directions as the kids tore into the gifts. Hopefully he'd recall the happy looks on their faces when the American Express bill arrived next month.

Yesterday Duke had suggested to Renée that they bring the kids together for a final reunion before Christmas. Bernice had offered to cook and had proposed that the kids decorate her tree and exchange gifts at her house. After phoning the Jensens, Renée had received permission for the Carter sisters to spend Saturday with the group. Early this morning they'd loaded the boys into Duke's truck and he'd followed Renée to the Jensens' where they'd collected Crystal and Evie, then drove to The Fridge—a refrigerated toboggan run in Waterford Oaks County Park.

Not only had the kids enjoyed the two one-thousand-foot flumes and a sledding hill, but he and Renée had had a blast. For five hours the kids had played as if the world was perfect, good and right. He'd even managed to sneak a kiss from Renée when they'd retreated inside Lookout Lodge to buy a round of hot chocolate for the group. The one person missing from their perfect day had been Timmy. Because of his pneumonia he'd stayed behind with Bernice.

When they'd returned from The Fridge late in the afternoon, a real Christmas tree, already strung with lights, stood in Bernice's front window. Extra gifts had been stuffed beneath the pine branches courtesy of Renée's brother, Rich, and his police officer buddies, who'd joined the group for dinner, then had departed to finish their shifts.

The camera flashed again—this time in Duke's eyes and he directed his best stop-that-or-else glare at Renée. Ignoring his threat, she smiled and snapped another picture. In a moment of sudden clarity, Duke realized the celebration might be the last of its kind for the kids, but he hoped only the beginning for him and Renée.

After tonight, Crystal and Evie would head to the Jensens'. Tomorrow, Willie and Ricci moved in with Mrs. Altman and then Renée planned to deliver José to the Covenant House. That left Timmy. Bernice had agreed to keep the boy with her until a bed became available at the children's home. The idea of being kid-free sent a surge of excitement through Duke. He eagerly anticipated focusing all his attention on Renée.

"Evie's turn," Timmy announced, handing the little girl a gift-wrapped box. "It's from all of us." The boy caught Duke's eye. "But Mr. D paid for it 'cause we didn't have any money."

Evie's eyes sparkled with excitement as she un-wrapped the box, then she squealed with delight when she saw the stuffed princess bear.

"It's the best gift I ever got, Timmy, thanks!" She hugged the bear, then approached Duke's chair. "Thank you, Mr. D." Evie opened her arms, leaving Duke no choice but to hug the little girl. After a gentle squeeze, he released her.

In need of air, Duke headed into the kitchen and straight to the sink, where he began washing a stack of dirty serving platters. The perfect day was winding down and Duke admitted he didn't want it to end. A few minutes later, Bernice invaded his privacy with an armload of dirty dishes from the dining-room table.

"Goodness, boys consume a lot of food," she said, piling the dishes on the counter. She stationed herself next to Duke and began drying the platters he'd scrubbed clean.

"I never expected it to be this difficult," he admitted. "They're just kids." He didn't have to explain himself. Bernice understood.

"Saying goodbye is never easy."

"I can't fathom how Renée handles this day in and day out."

"She's special."

The older woman would get no argument from him. In his opinion, Renée deserved a medal of honor for being a social worker. "People never talk about the thou-sands of children and teens living in cars, alleys or crumbling buildings across the country."

Bernice nodded.

"The average person never comes face-to-face with

the homeless. I've seen the pain, fear and need in their innocent eyes—" Duke swallowed hard and forged ahead "—but I never expected to feel guilty for the life I live." He shut off the tap and faced Renée's mother. "I'm ashamed to rest on clean sheets in a warm bed, because others are stuck dozing on sidewalks or park benches. I can't enjoy a hot shower because of those who are forced to bathe in public restrooms with cold water and paper towels. I get indigestion after having a T-bone steak because there's a kid out there somewhere digging through a Dumpster eating scraps from my meal."

"My dear, guilt is good."

"Guilt disturbs my sleep, Bernice. How can that be good?"

She patted his cheek. "Your sensitivity to the plight of the less fortunate will make you honest, generous and giving the rest of your days."

Renée's mother was right. Duke would support charities—if only to appease his guilty feelings. "It's easy to donate money. Renée's got the tough job."

"Speaking of my daughter…how are things between you two?"

Not sure what Renée had told her mother about their relationship, he played dumb. "What do you mean?"

Her eyes twinkled. "Have you kissed her?"

Boy, Bernice got right to the point. "Yes. I kissed her."

"And…?"

"We both liked it. A lot." He handed her a large mixing bowl.

"Then why the frown?" Bernice asked.

He'd never had a heart-to-heart with someone's mother, but Bernice was easy to talk to. "I don't believe Renée trusts me."

"Did she say as much?"

"No," Duke admitted, feeling foolish for speaking up.

"Be patient." Bernice offered a sympathetic smile. "My daughter's worth fighting for." She tossed the damp dish towel aside. "Anyone who earns her trust and love will discover she's loyal for life." Bernice left the kitchen.

"Mom said you needed help." Renée stood in the doorway a few moments later.

He swept an appreciative glance over her outfit. After the field trip to The Fridge, the females had showered and changed into dry clothes at Renée's while the guys had used Bernice's bathroom to wash up. The soft gray sweater turned her eyes cerulean in color. He decided that if he stared into those blue depths before he drifted off to sleep he'd never suffer from nightmares.

"Duke? Are you okay?"

Startled, he blinked. "Sure." He couldn't recall being this off balance before.

Renée confiscated a clean dish towel from the drawer.

"Are the kids finished opening gifts?" He hoped conversation would take his mind off the heady scent of her perfume—an earthy musk that spawned a fantasy of lounging with Renée beneath a willow tree along the banks of a trickling stream. Naked, of course.

"Mom put in the movie *A Christmas Story.* As soon as it ends, I'll drive the girls to the Jensens'."

"And I'll get the boys ready for bed," he offered.

"Actually," she began, her gaze sliding away. "Ricci and Willie get dropped off at Mrs. Altman's tomorrow." She paused. "Then I'm taking José to the Covenant House after." Her voice dropped. "And Mom's going to care for Timmy while I'm at work during the day."

He knew that already. A sharp pain lanced Duke's side. Was Renée trying to say goodbye?

"I'm at loose ends while the demolition's on hold,"

he argued. "No sense wearing out your mother when I'm capable of watching Timmy."

"You're doing enough, Duke. I don't want to impose on you anymore."

"Tell me you don't believe I consider those kids a nuisance."

"No," she whispered, head bent as she vigorously dried the gravy boat.

Needing to understand what he was fighting against, he asked, "Then why are you pushing me away?"

"You've done enough. More than you should have." Her dainty chin jutted. "I won't take advantage of your generosity."

There was more involved here than his wallet or his time. He searched her face, his stomach sinking at the steely determination in her stoic gaze. He wasn't ready to say goodbye to a woman who'd landed in his life unexpectedly, then slipped inside his heart when he hadn't been paying attention.

"I'll ride along with you when you deliver the girls to the Jensens'." That would give him an opportunity to convince Renée things were far from over between them.

She smiled, but for once her cute dimples failed to amuse him. "It will be easier if you don't make a big production of saying goodbye."

Renée knew more about kids than he did, so he'd abide by her request. But he wasn't letting *her* go without a big production. He was ticked. Damn ticked. They'd been dancing in circles since Renée had entered the kitchen. "What is it you're really trying to say?"

A feeling of unease crept across his shoulders when she fixated on her shoes. He'd been involved in plenty of business negotiations to sense an impending blow.

Renée didn't disappoint.

"It's best if you and me…" She snapped her mouth closed.

Each passing second of silence coincided with the thundering beat of his heart. "You and me what?"

"I like you, but—"

"Good." He swung her around. "I care a lot about you." He kissed her cheek, his lips lingering while he breathed in her scent. "We're not finished, Renée. We haven't even begun."

"Why?" she whispered, her eyes shimmering with tears.

Appalled that he'd upset her, he hugged her close. "God, sweetheart, I didn't mean to make you cry."

"Our worlds are polar opposites," she protested.

He had to kiss her to stop her from muttering stupid things. His mouth wooed her. Slow, steady and deep until her sweet sigh rolled across his lips. "Give me a chance to prove how good we are together."

The pleading in Duke's eyes tore at Renée. She understood exactly how he wanted to demonstrate that they were a perfect match. The past few days she'd dreamed of making love with him. Dreamed of pretending they had everything—instead of nothing—in common.

You deserve a little happiness. It had been so long since a man had…*dazzled* her.

If you can't have forever with Duke, then give yourself this night. A tiny miracle in the world of heartache that she lived and worked in.

"I'll tell my mother not to wait up for me after we drop off the girls."

His gaze smoldered as the meaning of her words sank in. "You're sure?"

"Positive." Certain she wanted to make love with Duke, but not convinced her heart would survive the experience.

"I'M NOT LETTING YOU change your mind," Duke promised the second he escorted her into his hotel room. In the blink of an eye, he pressed her against the closed door, then his mouth sank onto hers, chasing away second thoughts.

He controlled the kiss and as a result her emotions, which she gladly handed over to him for safekeeping. She trusted Duke would take good care of her. He sifted his fingers through her hair, pausing to knead her scalp. He broke off the kiss, his eyes asking, *Are we still okay?*

Between the door closing and his kiss, she'd lost her voice, so she ran her tongue over her lower lip in answer to his unspoken question. He flashed a boyish grin and laughter bubbled up her throat and poured out of her.

"You think it's funny that you've had me tied in knots for days?" He swooped her into his arms and three strides later dumped her in the middle of the bed, then pounced. Lying half on top of her, their chests pressed together, he sobered. "You should laugh more often. The sound is beautiful."

Dear Lord, Duke was good for her ego. "Do you usually joke around when you make love to a woman?"

"No. But you're special." He nuzzled a sensitive spot below her ear. "Very special." His mouth found hers in a soft, cherishing kiss that peeled away another layer of her defenses.

With ease he removed her clothes, save her knee-high leather boots. When she reached for the side zipper, he commanded, "Leave them on. They're sexy as hell."

Duke's assessing gaze made Renée self-conscious. "It's been a while for me," she confessed, feeling stupid and immature at revealing her insecurities.

"Good." He pressed his mouth to her ear. "Because I want you thinking about *me* when I'm inside you."

His words snatched her breath and she hooked her leg around his thigh, urging his body closer. "Why am I the only one who's naked?" she complained.

"I'll fix that right now."

She assisted him in tugging off his cowboy boots, then his sweater and finally his slacks. Then she wiggled her fingertips beneath the waistband of his boxers and spread her fingers across his muscular butt, giving a squeeze before he whisked away the offending article of clothing.

Oh, my.

The Oklahoma cowboy was going to take her on a ride she'd never been on before. He grinned devilishly, then attacked her—his hands everywhere at once, stroking, caressing, tickling, teasing. When his mouth joined in the fun, Renée relaxed and gave herself permission to bask in Duke's enthusiasm. Any lingering worries about taking this step with him evaporated in the steam of his kisses. No more fretting that this might be the biggest mistake of her life.

Freed from anxiety, Renée shoved against Duke's chest until he rolled to his back—right where she wanted him. She straddled his hips and rocked against his hardness, needing to appease the burning sensation in her belly. Oblivious to her distress, he played with her breasts, touching, caressing, tweaking, sucking.

Then he touched her hot core and she lifted her hips. Begging. The pressure of his fingers increased and her breathing accelerated. Needing to show him that she appreciated the care he took in arousing and pleasuring her, she pressed her mouth to his, pouring her heart into the kiss.

"You know what I admire most about you?" Duke whispered.

She raised an eyebrow.

"Your courage." His awe humbled her.

No one had ever labeled her courageous. She'd been told she was lucky. Lucky to be alive. Lucky her brother had found her. Lucky Bernice had taken her in. Lucky, lucky, lucky.

"I've never seen a person confront the obstacles you do on a day-to-day basis and not give up and walk away." He shoved a muscular thigh between her legs, then trailed kisses across her collarbone…over her breasts…her stomach…

His mouth tormented and teased bringing her close to the edge, then yanking her back. After several see-sawing experiences, he rummaged through the night-stand drawer and produced an unopened box of condoms. "Before you ask…" he said.

"I wasn't going to." Because she didn't want to hear about any other women in his life—past or present.

"But you should," he insisted, kissing the corner of her mouth. "I bought the condoms after our first kiss." His face drew closer. "I knew then that I wanted to make love with you." He kissed her again, then asked, "Has there ever been anyone special for you?"

Her chest ached that a man like Duke needed reassurance. She rubbed her fingertips against the day-old whiskers along his jaw. "He was a long time ago."

"How long?" Duke pressed.

"College."

"And…?"

"In the end we'd decided that we weren't the right match after all." Almost the truth—it had been Sean's parents who'd determined she wasn't fit for their son.

"I'm glad it didn't work out." He brushed a kiss against her forehead. "Because if it had, I'd have missed this moment with you." He kissed her until her toes tingled.

"Make me yours," she begged, arching her hips.

Now...this moment...would be her only *forever* with Duke.

Given the green light, he grabbed a condom and sheathed himself. Pinning her wrists to the pillow beneath her head, he clasped her hands. Eyes open, gazes clinging, he slid inside her. She eagerly met his thrusts. Breathing became impossible, not because his mouth smothered her with kisses, but because she held her breath as he lifted her higher...higher...higher...

Hovering on the brink of insanity, she wrapped her legs around his waist and dug her boot heels into his hips, demanding he thrust harder and faster.

The end pulled the last of the oxygen from her lungs and sent her tumbling head over boot heels into oblivion.

Chapter Eleven

Duke rolled over in bed expecting to bump into a warm body, but instead encountered cold sheets. His eyes popped open and searched the room for Renée. The soft glow from the city lights spilled through the floor-to-ceiling windows, illuminating the solitary figure poised in front of them. Wearing only Duke's dress shirt, Renée hugged her waist, her profile pensive and resolute as she stared at the iced-over Detroit River.

They'd spent an incredible three hours feasting on each other before they'd succumbed to exhaustion. That he'd awoken to find the woman of his fantasies frowning bruised his ego. He slipped from the bed, padded across the carpet and wrapped his arms around her waist, resting his chin on the top of her head. The scent of her sleepy body stirred him. Amazing. Even now, after she'd drained him, a certain part of his anatomy stirred, ready for another round of lovemaking. "What's caught your attention?"

"From way up here the area looks serene. Beautiful. And good." She pressed her fingertips to the cold glass. "Exactly how the city hopes tourists will view Detroit when they visit."

He sensed a *but* coming…

"But I see only ramshackle buildings and houses, dangerous alleys and city parks where the homeless wait for miracles."

As if he shared her pain, Duke battled a strong need to right the wrongs in her world. This desire to protect her from the ugliness she dealt with day in and day out proved he was falling in love with Renée. He nuzzled her neck. "You're their miracle."

"I try so hard, Duke, but it's never enough."

Their faces reflected in the glass. Hers—tight with worry. His—sober with concern that after Renée gave her all to the needy, there'd be nothing left for him. How did a man compete against those less fortunate?

The bedside clock flashed 3:00 a.m. Too early to contemplate the future, but the perfect time to help Renée forget her troubles. The city might own her during the day, many evenings and even occasional weekends, but right now she was his. He trailed kisses along her neck, then dipped beneath the shirt collar to nibble her shoulder. "What do you say we try out the Jacuzzi tub in the bathroom?"

"Mmm." She spun, wrapped her arms around his neck and offered her mouth. "I say, yes." He kissed her. Over. And over. Until they were both light-headed and off balance. Her fingers threaded through his mussed hair. The scrape of her nails against his scalp made him shiver, then he groaned in pleasure when she peppered his face with light kisses.

"C'mon." He tugged her hand. "Before we get carried away and end up making love on the carpet in front of the windows."

Eyes sparkling with mischief she glanced at the windows, then quirked an eyebrow.

Well, well, the social worker had a sense of adventure.

He spread the blanket from the bed across the carpet and made sure the box of condoms was within reach. Then he dropped to his knees and held out his hand. She shed his shirt before joining him. They stretched out in front of the window, him behind her, rubbing against her warmth as they stared across the river.

He palmed her breasts; the pleasure on her face reflected in the glass more erotic than anything he'd ever experienced. She pushed her bottom against his stomach, her fingers clutching his thigh. Already aroused, he focused on making Renée squirm.

Her body arched, seeking fulfillment—pleasure only he could give her. Hands caressed and teased. Lips courted.

"I want you inside me, Duke." She curled her fingers around his erection.

And that's where he wanted to be—always. He sheathed himself and went a little crazy when he found her wet and ready. He rolled on top of her, feasting on her breasts. Her stomach. The blond curls between her thighs.

Her kisses tasted of desperation and stirred a feeling of panic in Duke. Before he made sense of the emotion, Renée sent him over the edge to an explosive climax as dark and mysterious as the Detroit night.

COLD SHEETS AGAIN?

After making love in front of the windows, Duke had carried Renée to the bed and they'd drifted off to sleep, with her promise to explore the Jacuzzi after a short nap. He cracked open an eye and peeked at the clock: 9:00 a.m. A quick glance around confirmed Renée wasn't in the room. Maybe the bathroom—he tuned his ears and listened. Nothing. He sat up, fighting the queasiness churning in his gut. Her coat was gone from the chair where he'd tossed it last night. As were her pants, sweater and the sexy high-heeled boots.

She'd snuck out.

He swung his feet to the floor and rested his head in his hands.

Maybe she'd received a call from her mother needing help with the boys.

Maybe her boss phoned with an emergency.

Maybe she hadn't been feeling well.

Or maybe she'd left to fetch them breakfast. *Yeah, that's it.* He hurried into the bathroom to grab a quick shower. First, he needed to shave. He flipped on the hot water tap, then froze when he spotted the note propped against his grooming kit.

His stomach bottomed out and his lungs squeezed until his breathing became a wheeze.

Shit.

A Dear Duke letter. He cursed his trembling hand as he scanned the hotel stationery.

> Duke…last night was amazing. You're a very
> special man.

What the hell? He gripped the paper tighter as if his hold would choke the words until they faded.

> I can't thank you enough for what you've done
> to help our kids.

His throat ached. José, Crystal, Evie, Ricci, Willie and Timmy. They were his kids, as well as Renée's, weren't they?

> I'll never forget you. Renée.

That's it? Just *Renée?* No...*Call me.* No...*See you soon?*

Fricking unbelievable. He crumpled the paper and pitched it at the mirror. She'd used him, damn it. She'd gotten what she'd wanted—help with the kids and a roll in the hay—now he served no purpose. If she intended to call it quits, the least she could do was tell him to get lost face-to-face instead of taking the coward's way out.

He hopped into the shower and scrubbed himself hard—leaving his skin raw and chaffed. He dried off, tossed on a pair of jeans and a sweater, then his boots and was halfway to the door before he put on the brakes.

What are you doing?

Renée wasn't a businessman or client he could bully until she changed her mind. He paced across the floor and stood before the windows, studying the frozen landscape in the light of day. Last night had been the first time he and Renée had been alone without the kids. Maybe the experience had overwhelmed her. Hell, their lovemaking had knocked him off-kilter. Was she running scared? Or did she need breathing room to adjust to the change in their relationship?

He'd allow her time to sort through her feelings. If he didn't hear from her later today, he'd stop by her office tomorrow and offer to take her to lunch. Once he had her alone, he'd use every power in his possession to convince her that making love was the beginning, not the end of them as a couple.

In the meantime, he resigned himself to a day of room service and Sunday sports programming.

Rah, rah, rah.

A LOUD NOISE startled Duke and he shot out of the chair. Disoriented, he checked his watch. 5:00 p.m. He must have dozed off during the football game.

A knock at the door startled him again. "Duke?"

Renée? Thank God. He'd jumped to conclusions after all. The note she'd left in the bathroom this morning hadn't been a Dear Duke letter. He felt like an ass—a grinning ass as he rushed to the door. "Hey."

Her gaze skipped over his face and landed on his shoulder.

"What's wrong?" When he motioned for her to enter the hotel room, she remained rooted to the carpet in the hallway. His sense of relief dissipated.

"We've got a problem."

We?

She glanced over her shoulder and Duke poked his head out the door to see what had snagged her attention. At the far end of the corridor out of earshot, José lounged against the wall near the elevator, a duffel bag resting at his feet.

Evidently makeup sex was out of the question. "What's going on?"

In hushed words she explained, "Earlier today I delivered Ricci and Willie to Mrs. Altman's. Everything went fine." She rubbed her forehead. "When I returned home to drive José to the Covenant House, he threatened to go back to the streets."

Duke's gaze veered to José. The teen's I-don't-give-a-damn-about-the-world glare convinced Duke the boy was scared.

"He'll be okay once he sees the place." Duke wasn't sure who the words were meant to reassure—him or Renée.

"I agree. The problem is getting him there." Finally

she made eye contact—he wished she hadn't. Her eyes were brimming with misery—misery over the way she'd ditched him the previous night or was her concern solely for José? "I hoped if you accompanied us, José would be more cooperative."

Dumping a kid off at a group home was out of Duke's area of expertise. Besides, he didn't deserve to be the bad guy and that's exactly what he'd be if he went along for the ride.

"I realize this is a lot to ask, but…" She sucked in a deep breath. "José needs you."

Sensing Renée needed him, too, Duke shoved his fingers through his hair and swallowed a curse. How had everything become so complicated? All he'd wanted was for the kids to be gone from his warehouse and stashed somewhere safe, enabling him to go about the business of relocating his company. Feeling cornered, he grumbled, "Give me a second." Then he shut the door in her face—not something a gentleman would do, but he wasn't feeling gallant at the moment.

Five minutes later the group rode the elevator in silence to the motor-coach level, then walked outside and crossed the street to the parking garage where Duke's truck sat. The drive to Martin Luther King Jr. Boulevard took eight minutes—four-hundred-eight seconds of additional silence.

The Covenant House was a 5.3-acre gated campus that housed two residential programs, a community center and administrative offices. Renée directed Duke to the parking lot in front of the residential hall where José would temporarily make his home.

Renée twisted in her seat to speak to the teen. "Feel free to look around inside while I register you with the director." She left the truck and hurried to a side entrance, where she used a key card to enter the building.

Obviously the teen was in no rush to investigate the premises. Duke allowed the engine to run and switched the heat to low. He glanced in the rearview mirror and the desolate expression on José's face tempted Duke to shift into reverse and take off—anywhere that would erase the bleakness from the kid's eyes.

Staring out the windshield at the black chain-link fence that surrounded the property, Duke said, "It's okay to be nervous."

José punched the seat with his fist and spat, "You should've left us alone. We were fine in that warehouse."

Duke guessed he'd feel the same if he'd been separated from those he considered family. "Fine for how long?" he asked. "Until one of you became ill? A drunk attacked your group? Or a gang discovered your hideout and demanded it for themselves?"

"Nothin' would have happened to us," José argued, though with less conviction.

It wasn't fair that the other kids had found homes together while José and eventually Timmy had to go off on their own. "Being a man isn't always easy." His comment caught José's attention. "Sometimes being a man means facing the future alone. And trusting yourself to make good decisions." He cleared his throat. "And the others will be watching you."

"Huh?"

"Ricci, Willie and Timmy. They admire you and they'll follow your example because they trust you. If they hear that you're living on the streets again, they'll run off and try to find you."

"That's bullshit." Angry eyes glared at Duke. "They've got real homes now. That's all they care about."

"You're wrong," Duke argued. "They won't forget what you did for them. You made sure they were safe. Now you need to consider what's best for you and your future."

"Some future," he muttered.

"The future is what you make of it." Duke removed a business card from his wallet. "Call me anytime you want to talk."

"Talk about what?" José grumbled but accepted the card.

"Sports…girls…school. Anything." After a moment he asked, "What do you say we go in?"

Bag in hand José left the truck. They entered through the main doors into a recreation room. Duke caught the flash of surprise in José's eyes when the two young men playing Ping-Pong waved. One resident sprawled across a couch in front of a TV and two girls studied at a table in the corner. Vending machines lined a wall and a humungous bowl of fruit sat on the administrator's desk.

"May I help you?" An older man with long gray sideburns strolled into the room.

Duke offered his hand. "Duke Dalton. This is José." He nudged the teen's side and the boy shook the man's hand. "José's a new resident. Renée Sweeney is registering him."

"I'm Scott, the senior administrator. Welcome to Covenant House, José. We've got a room ready for you."

Right then a muscular bald man covered in tattoos from neck to knuckles roared, "This one's mine!"

Tattoo-man grinned. "José, right?" A beefy hand inched toward the boy. "They call me the Beast. But I also go by Roger."

José reluctantly offered his hand.

"I heard you were a hero," Roger said.

The teen's eyes rounded, but he neither confirmed nor denied the charge.

"Ms. Sweeney said you took care of a bunch of homeless kids in a warehouse along the Riverfront. A lot of bad stuff goes on there."

Unimpressed with the praise, José shrugged.

"We need more guys like you," Roger said. "If you're interested we'll train you for our street outreach program while you're here."

"What's that?" José finally spoke.

"A group of our residents drive a van through the toughest neighborhoods in Detroit, searching for kids who need help. We try to convince them that they don't have to live on the streets or hang with gangs. And if they're willing, we bring them here, then try to get them the help they need."

"What would I have to do?" José asked.

"Talk to kids your age. Get them to trust you. Convince them that there's a better way to live. We hand out food, hygiene kits and other supplies. We've been doing this for a few years now. When kids on the street see our van they recognize we're there to help."

"So you don't make them go to a shelter?"

"We don't make them do anything they don't want to."

"I'll think about it," José murmured.

"Ready to meet your roommate?" Roger led them through a maze of halls that reminded Duke of a college dormitory. Tattooed knuckles rapped against a door next to the stairwell. "Hey, Rambo, your roomie's here."

Rambo? Duke and José exchanged surprised glances. Was the teen bunking with a cage fighter?

Rambo turned out to be a skinny, white eighteen-year-old with Coke-bottle glasses and a shy smile.

"This is Rambo, aka Kenny."

"Hey," José grumbled.

Kenny motioned to the empty twin bed and Duke noticed the scars on the boy's wrists. How long ago had he attempted suicide? "I heard you were coming so I bought you a candy bar," Kenny said.

Surprised, José mumbled, "Thanks." He tossed his duffel onto the bed, then studied the pencil sketches taped to the cinder block wall above the built-in desk. "Those yours?" He inched closer.

"Yeah, they aren't any good but—"

"They're awesome, dude." Another step closer.

"Do you draw?" Kenny shoved his glasses up the bridge of his nose.

"No, man. I can't draw worth shit." Then he asked, "You play any sports?"

"I like basketball."

"Me, too."

Kenny's face brightened. "Cool."

"Maybe you can teach me to draw. There's this girl…" José glanced at Duke, then shrugged. "Never mind."

"You want to eat? Supper's at six o'clock."

"Go ahead," Duke encouraged.

"It's pizza night." Kenny walked out of the room.

At the doorway José paused, but didn't speak.

Throat tight, Duke said, "You've got my number." He didn't want to embarrass the teen with a hug, so he clasped his shoulder.

José nodded, then followed his roommate. Duke heard José ask, "You ever been to a Red Wings game?"

"José seems like a decent kid," Roger commented.

Duke agreed.

"He'll be assigned chores like the others and have an opportunity to earn spending money for the vending machines or other items the house doesn't provide. We use a debit card system."

"If it's allowed, I'll add money to his card to tie him over until he gets paid."

"That's why I told you. Stop at the front desk and ask for Miranda. She'll open José's account."

"Thanks."

"If Renée can't find José a foster home, we'll enroll him in a program to earn his GED. Everyone who lives here has to take a training course that will help them land a job." Roger paused in the doorway. "We'll take good care of him." Then he was gone, leaving Duke to study the teen's new home—two single beds, one dresser, a shared nightstand and desk. Better than a cardboard box. And José wouldn't be alone. He had Rambo now. They'd watch out for each other.

But who would take care of Renée?

DARN IT.

Renée should have suggested they take separate vehicles to the Covenant House. Now she was stuck riding with Duke to the hotel to retrieve her station wagon. Lord, the things she did for kids.

She studied the passing scenery—not much discernable in the dark, but the activity prevented her eyes from straying to Duke's face. She hadn't expected to see him so soon after making love. If not for José's rebellion, she would have avoided the man as long as possible.

Yes, she was a coward.

The previous night in Duke's arms had been incredible. What frightened her most wasn't the great sex, but the emotional connection she'd experienced with him. She'd given him more than her heart—she'd given him her trust and that worried her deeply.

Her former fiancé, Sean, served as a reminder of her naiveté. She'd trusted that his love for her would enable him to stand up to his parents. Instead, he'd decided their relationship hadn't been worth fighting for.

What if Duke arrived at the same conclusion as Sean? She'd shatter into a million pieces if Duke believed she wasn't worth the hassle.

She'd taken the coward's way out—sneaking off at the break of dawn. Duke deserved better. Because of his cooperation, her boss hadn't learned about the kids' plight and Renée's unconventional handling of the situation, saving her from reprimands or worse—losing her job.

"Have you eaten?" he asked.

"No."

Instead of driving to the hotel parking lot, he went to Mammy's Café. At six-thirty there wasn't a wait. May had the day off so another hostess seated them in a booth, filled their water glasses, handed over menus and left with the promise that a waitress would take their orders shortly.

When Renée gathered the courage to glance at Duke her nerves tightened painfully. She'd expected anger or hurt, not concern in his gaze—thoughtfulness Renée didn't deserve. He put aside the menu and said, "I'll take whatever you're having."

The waitress arrived and Renée requested the meat-loaf special with mashed potatoes and gravy. Then she apologized. "About the note. I panicked." She winced at her feeble attempt. "I got in over my head and I didn't know how to…" *Get out.*

He threaded his fingers through hers, his callused palm reminding her of his hands gliding over her bare hip…her leg…her breast. "What we shared was special,

Renée. I admit it blew me away, too. Don't be frightened of your feelings."

She didn't dare allow her feelings for Duke to grow. As much as she yearned to experience the magic of his touch day after day, she refused to use him. And that's what she'd end up doing because she had nothing to offer Duke but an affair.

"I have a proposition for you," he said. "Fly home with me to Tulsa for Christmas."

"What?"

"I'd like you to meet my family."

Her heart doubled its beat, panicking at the idea of mingling with Duke's siblings and stepfather. "Timmy won't be in a home by Christmas." She didn't have the heart to put the boy in an orphanage until after the holidays. Renée intended for Timmy to spend Christmas with her and Bernice.

"We'll bring Timmy along. My brother rodeos and he'll teach the kid how to throw a rope. And Sam will show him how to ride and—"

Renée pulled her hand free. "I can't leave my mom or Rich alone on Christmas. We always spend the holiday together." Christmas was Renée's birthday—a very special day for her brother and mother.

"What if we fly out tomorrow and return to Detroit Christmas Eve day?"

A part of her yearned to accompany Duke to make up for the horrible way she'd left him after an incredible night of lovemaking. And if she was brutally honest with herself, she'd admit to a curiosity about the Cartwrights. What if they were different from the wealthy people she'd dealt with? Did she dare walk away from Duke before she was certain their worlds didn't stand a chance of coexisting? "How much would the airfare be?"

"Airfare is complimentary. My stepfather will send his private jet."

Private jet set off warning bells in her head. *Relax, Renée. Give him a chance.* She had a full week of vacation left this year and doubted her boss would deny Renée's request for a few days off.

He pressed her fingertips to his mouth. "Please."

Don't make him beg. He's done so much for you and the kids.

"When do we leave?"

Chapter Twelve

"Is your brother a real cowboy, Mr. D?"

"Yep. He's as real as they come, Timmy."

The pair stood on the front porch of the ranch house, watching Duke's stepbrother, clothed in a long duster, cowboy hat, boots and thick winter gloves ride in against a backdrop of dark clouds brewing along the horizon. A snowstorm—or worse, ice storm—had its sights on Tulsa. He hoped the weather wouldn't interfere with his promise to fly Renée and Timmy home by Christmas Eve day.

Matt halted the horse a few feet from the porch. Face red from the blowing wind, he grinned. "Heard you were visiting for a couple of days."

"This is Timmy." Duke squeezed the boy's shoulder. "Timmy, this is my brother, the rodeo star, Mr. Cartwright."

"Call me Matt. Mr. Cartwright's my dad." The cowboy made a silly face and Timmy giggled. Matt looked at Duke. "I assume Sam told you about my win in Pocatello."

"Yep. And that you're starting up a horse-breeding operation."

"Our sister's got a big mouth."

"What's your horse's name, Mr. Matt?" Timmy interrupted the adults.

"Leroy."

"That's a weird name for a horse."

"Well, Leroy is a weird horse. Want to discover why and ride with me to the barn?"

Timmy glanced at Duke, yearning in his eyes. "Can I, Mr. D?"

"Sure." He directed his next words to Matt. "Keep a close eye on him."

When Timmy descended the steps, dragging his foot behind him, understanding dawned on Matt's face. Duke followed, then arranged Timmy sideway in the saddle.

A click of Matt's tongue sent Leroy in the direction of the barn, Timmy clutching the saddle horn, a nervous smile on his face. Duke retreated inside the house where Renée helped Sam and the Cartwright housekeeper, Juanita, prepare supper. His stepfather, Dominick, happened to be out of town on business until tomorrow.

The smell of frying chicken teased Duke's nose as he walked toward the kitchen. He hovered in the doorway, observing the three women. Renée stood out like a sore thumb—a beautiful sore thumb—among the dark-haired, dark-skinned women in the room. Juanita manned the stove, turning chicken pieces in the hot grease while chatting about her grandson's church play later in the evening. Sam washed and sliced vegetables at the kitchen sink. Renée set the table.

"Juanita, you better leave if you wish to be on time for Ricardo's play," Sam said. "Renée and I can manage supper."

When the grandmotherly woman protested, Duke spoke. "I'll help." He winked at the housekeeper. "I'm not useless in the kitchen."

Sam stuck out her tongue, but Duke ignored the taunt. It was a well-known fact that his stepsister had difficulty boiling water and Duke was able to cook enough food to feed a bunkhouse full of cowboys—thanks to Juanita's teachings. When Duke and his mother had arrived at the ranch, the housekeeper had noticed how little time Duke's mother had spent with him. Juanita had taken him under her wing and put him to work in the kitchen assisting her.

Rising on tiptoe, Juanita patted Duke's cheek. "If you watch over these two, I will go."

Sam snorted, but there was a note of affection behind the sound.

Juanita clasped Renée's hands. "Tomorrow Timmy and I will bake cookies." Sam helped the older woman with her coat, then escorted her outside.

Left alone in the kitchen with Renée, Duke searched for a conversation starter, when what he really wanted to do was kiss her. She'd been quiet on the flight to Tulsa, but Timmy had eased the tension with a hundred questions about airplanes and flying—most of which Duke hadn't been able to answer.

"Where's Timmy?" Renée glanced toward the kitchen doorway.

"He's helping Matt feed Leroy." At her concerned expression he assured, "Don't worry. My brother's good with animals. He'll keep Timmy safe."

"Your sister is lovely, Duke." Renée folded paper napkins, placing one next to each plate.

"Yeah, she is." Had his stepsister spoken about her injury? Or did Renée notice Sam was a bit *off*?

As if Renée read his mind, she said, "Sam mentioned the accident." Renée expelled a soft breath. "It's terrible that she feels the need to apologize for repeating herself."

"Once Sam becomes comfortable with you, she'll relax." He suspected Sam hoped to make a good impression because Duke cared about Renée. If only his stepsister would stop attempting to please others and concentrate on making herself happy.

"Sam says her father drives her crazy because he's overprotective."

Not wanting to discuss his stepsister or Dominick, Duke closed the gap between them to within touching distance. "Tomorrow I'll give you a tour of the ranch."

"Not on horseback, I hope." She made a funny face. "I'm a city girl, Duke. Horses scare me more than rottweilers."

He brushed a finger across her cheek, lingering at the corner of her mouth. He loved the way her blue eyes drifted to his lips. She wanted him to kiss her.

"I'm not much for the ranching life, but Sam shamed me into learning how to ride." He puffed up. "And Matt taught me the art of lassoing a calf."

"Braggart." Renée's gaze remained hot and needy.

Duke bent his head and she met him halfway. A gentle brushing of lips. He ran his tongue across her lower lip and she sighed, opening her mouth wider. He wrapped her tight in his arms and the feel of her soft breasts bumping his chest sparked an erotic fantasy in his head. He stroked Renée's fanny, then cupped her breast, then—

Bam! The door flew open and Duke jerked away from Renée.

"Mr. D! I fed Leroy and guess what?"

"What?" Duke rasped, ignoring the startled expression on his stepbrother's face.

"Leroy licked my face like a dog." Timmy giggled, the adults joining in the laughter.

"Who's our lovely guest?" Matt's eyes hadn't left

Renée. His stepbrother was a notorious ladies' man. Duke observed Renée's reaction, fearing she'd join the hundreds of rodeo groupies who'd succumbed to his stepbrother's charm over the years.

"You're as pretty as an Oklahoma sunset." Matt lifted Renée's hand and kissed her knuckles, then cast a sideway glance at Duke. "If you're wanting a cowboy, ma'am, I'm the real thing. Duke just dresses like one."

Sam made a gagging sound as she joined the group in the kitchen and Duke was pleased when Renée rolled her eyes.

"Renée Sweeney." She pulled her hand from his grasp. "Pleasure to meet you, Matt."

"Welcome to the Lazy River. I'd be happy to show you around the ranch, or has my brother beaten me to the punch?"

"Duke beat you," Renée answered in a no-nonsense tone.

"Matt, play nice, or Duke and I will kick you out of the sandbox." Sam stepped next to Renée and whispered, "Stick with Duke. You're better off with a corporate cowboy than a real one with commitment issues."

"This kid's got a way with animals. Leroy took to him right away." Matt ruffled Timmy's hair.

Timmy wandered over to Renée and leaned against her side, smiling shyly at the adults. The kid must be exhausted after all the excitement of the day.

Supper was loud and entertaining as Matt regaled the group with rodeo stories. Timmy cleaned his plate, but Duke doubted the boy even tasted the food, too caught up in Matt's steer-roping tales. Renée remained quiet, casting glances at Duke, making him yearn for an excuse to go off alone with her.

"The girls cooked. Guys have to clean the kitchen,"

Sam announced. "C'mon, Timmy. I'll help you get your bath ready."

"I'll be right there," Renée promised, taking a handful of dishes to the sink. Duke's cell phone went off and he excused himself to answer the call in his stepfather's office.

Left alone with Matt, Renée said, "I'll wash if you dry and put away."

"Forget the dishes. Have a seat while I start the coffee."

As Matt measured coffee grounds, Renée asked, "How large is the Lazy River Ranch?"

"Over ten thousand acres." He flipped the switch on the coffeemaker, then joined her at the table. "Has Duke told you much about his family?"

"He mentioned your father prefers oil over cattle."

"The old man detests cows. The bovines around here are for show. My father pretends he gives a damn about cows, that way if he decides to enter into politics one day he won't have made enemies with the local ranchers."

"How did you end up rodeoing for a living?"

"Like any hotheaded young kid I joined the circuit because my father didn't approve. Not sure who was more surprised—me or him—when I ended up being damned good at the sport."

"And Duke didn't tag along with you?"

Matt burst out laughing. "Duke hated the ranch when he first arrived. Spent most of his days with his head buried in books or hanging out in the kitchen with Juanita. My father's always been impressed by Duke's savvy business sense. But Duke wants nothing to do with Cartwright oil."

"Who helps your father run his company?"

"Sam works in the office. In truth, I'd rather muck out stalls than sit at a desk and watch the price of oil fluctuate every two minutes."

The coffeemaker timer rang and Matt got up from the

table. "I'm contemplating a career change. When the time is right I'll take the money in my trust fund and head out on my own like Duke did."

"Duke received a trust fund from your father?" As soon as she'd spoken, Renée wished to rescind the question. Now Matt would believe she was interested in Duke's money when in fact she viewed the Cartwright fortune as a major obstacle between them.

"My brother refused the trust fund. His company's success can be attributed to Duke's hard work and sound business decisions." Matt delivered the coffee mugs to the table.

"Why wouldn't Duke take the money?"

"He wants to be his own man. I understand that. I'm feeling the itch to break away from my father's control, too. And I may have found a way." Matt blew across the top of his mug. "Might enter into the horse-breeding business."

"Let me guess." Renée smiled. "Your father doesn't appreciate horses any better than cows?"

"Bingo. Duke made the right decision in moving his company."

"How so?"

"Ever since his mother died, my father's become worse about sticking his nose into our lives. He's disappointed none of us have taken an interest in oil."

Renée made a noncommittal sound.

"No offense, but we were shocked when Duke announced the new location of his company."

She was used to people dissing the Motor City. "Detroit isn't as bad as it's made out to be in TV shows and movies. People who live there are survivors. Even if it takes years, they'll fight to restore the city to its glory days."

"Mind if I ask what's going on between you and my brother?"

"Duke's been helping me care for a group of homeless kids that were living in his warehouse." That was the truth, although she suspected Matt's question had been aimed toward her and Duke's personal relationship.

"Sam said you were a social worker."

Renée nodded. "Timmy's the last in the group who needs a home."

"I wasn't aware that social workers took kids on trips with them."

Her face heated. "Technically I'm breaking the rules. But Timmy's a special case."

"He's a nice boy. What's his story?"

"The usual. He was born to a teenage mother. She didn't want to deal with his medical issues, so she gave him up. He entered into the foster care system, but has never been adopted nor has he received the proper care for his club foot."

"Will you eventually find a family to take him in?"

"His chances aren't good. After Christmas he'll be given a bed in an orphanage."

"What happens between you and Duke once Timmy's situated?"

The million-dollar question—not surprising from the son of a millionaire. She flashed a smile that she hoped was convincing. "We're just friends."

"Friends who sleep together?" Matt grinned devilishly when she gasped. "Don't worry, he didn't tell me. I guessed."

"Please don't get any ideas. It's not—"

"'Bout time a woman's caught my brother's attention. Duke was becoming a boring—"

"Talking about me?" Duke strolled into the kitchen.

"Ears burning?" Matt guzzled the rest of his coffee, then set the mug in the sink. "You help your beautiful *senorita* wash dishes. I'm heading into town to have fun before Dad arrives tomorrow and we have to sit around the Christmas tree and make nice with each other." He winked at Renée, then grabbed his coat and swaggered out of the house.

"Boring, huh?" Duke muttered.

Taking pity on him, Renée assured, "You're far from being a dud." That was the problem. Duke was a man with principles—a man who demanded the respect of others. He was caring, solicitous and concerned about homeless kids. Add in sex appeal and handsomeness and he reached perfection.

He walked behind her chair and massaged her shoulders, then whispered in her ear, "Will you sit with me in front of the fire tonight and let me bore you?"

Renée couldn't imagine anything better than a cozy fire and a boring Duke.

"WELCOME HOME, DOMINICK." Duke's greeting carried through the hall, turned the corner and smacked into Renée. She froze, unsure whether to retreat upstairs or eavesdrop a few minutes before joining the men in the kitchen. The smell of brewing coffee teased her nose. *Eavesdrop* won hands-down.

"Duke, my boy. Glad you decided to stop in for the holidays."

A thudding sound echoed in the air and she assumed the two men had engaged in manly backslaps.

"How's the Detroit project going?"

"Good. Ran into a snag, but that's been resolved."

"What kind of problem—worker shortage, equipment or permits trouble?"

Oh…just six homeless kids living in the building.

Before Duke had the opportunity to answer, his stepfather sounded off again. "If you're in over your head, you've got your trust fund."

"I appreciate that, Dominick, but I built in several corners that I can cut if cost becomes an issue."

Renée hated the idea that helping her out might impact Dalton Industries' financial health.

"Anytime you need investors I'd be happy to call in a few favors," Dominick offered.

One of the things she'd learned dealing with the community development board had been that people with money spent much of their time forming connections with others like themselves. A tight-knit, impenetrable circle of greed that controlled all things connected to their rich world.

"Thanks for the offer, but I've had a few investors express interest already."

Renée was proud of Duke for standing his ground with his stepfather and resisting the temptation to take the easy way out.

"If I didn't admire you so much, Duke, I'd be tempted to wring your neck for snubbing my help and my money. I loved your mother and I consider you my son the same as Matt."

"Dominick, I—"

"—have to do this your way. Promise me that if you find yourself in a situation I can help with, you'll allow me to."

Before Duke answered, his stepfather said, "Who are you?"

Startled she leaned over the banister, but the kitchen remained out of view.

"Timmy."

"Timmy what?" Dominick demanded.

"Timmy McFadden. Who are you?"

"Dominick Cartwright."

"Are you Mr. D's dad?"

"Who's Mr. D?"

Renée envisioned the boy pointing to Duke.

"Duke's my stepson."

The sound of a chair scraping the floor told her that Timmy had seated himself at the table. "What's a stepson?"

"Duke's real father died and his mother married me, so I became his stepdad." Then Dominick asked, "Who's your dad?"

"I don't got one."

"What do you mean you don't have a father?"

"Timmy doesn't have a dad right at the moment," Duke cut in.

"Ms. Sweeney's trying to find me one."

Renée cringed, fearing another round of questions.

"Who's Ms. Sweeney?"

"Mr. D's girlfriend."

She sucked in a quiet breath, wishing she was able to see Duke's face.

"Ms. Sweeney is your mother?"

"No, silly. She's… Mr. D, what's Ms. Sweeney again?"

"She's a social worker for the city of Detroit. She helps find homes for kids who don't have them."

"Yeah, like me. Ms. Sweeney already found a home for Crystal and Evie. Then she found Mrs. Altman who said she'd take Ricci and Willie. And José got to go to this place for teenagers."

"You have that many brothers and sisters?" Dominick asked.

"We're not brothers and sisters. Well, Crystal and Evie are sisters, but the rest of us are friends. We used to live in Mr. D's warehouse. Right, Mr. D?"

"Homeless kids camped out in your building?"

Renée detected a note of outrage in the older man's question and wondered if it was more for show or if he truly believed the children's situation despicable.

Duke cautioned, "It's a long story, Dominick."

The warning went unheeded. "Why were you living in my stepson's building?"

"'Cause José said I could. He was there first."

"Then where did you come from?"

"José found me digging in the Dumpster outside Tony's Pizza. They got the best pizza in the whole world."

"Why were you digging in a Dumpster?"

"I ran away from my foster home and I was hungry."

"Why did you run away?"

Good grief! Was this a game of twenty questions?

"Mr. Polanski was mean and he kept making fun of how I walked."

Renée pictured Timmy's chin jutting in the air. She'd investigated the boy's claims of mistreatment after she'd discovered him at the warehouse. Mr. Polanski and his wife, Eleanor, had several complaints of verbal abuse against them in their file. But many times social workers looked the other way, assuming a child was better off being yelled at than living on the streets.

"Then I should punch Mr. Polanski in the nose."

Her heart melted at Dominick's words. Had she jumped to conclusions about the millionaire? He might be opinionated and stubborn—most older men were— but she sensed that Dominick had a soft spot for the less fortunate.

"You should punch Mr. Polanski in his big fat belly," Timmy said. "That would hurt."

The men chuckled, then Duke spoke. "Timmy has a knack for mathematics, don't you?"

"Ms. Sweeney brings me workbooks and I do the problems all by myself."

"You should be in school," Dominick scolded.

"I get to go to school when Ms. Sweeney finds me a foster family."

"So you think Mr. D likes Ms. Sweeney?" Dominick asked.

"Yeah. He stayed overnight at her house when I got sick and we played NASCAR games 'cause Mr. D bought an Xbox for the TV."

"You don't say?"

Renée's cheeks heated at Dominick's curiosity.

"And Mr. D took us to a hockey game and we had pizza and licorice. I got a bobblehead, too, and he bought Ms. Sweeney a jersey."

"Sounds like you have a lot of fun with Mr. D."

"Yep." Without missing a beat, Timmy announced, "I'm hungry."

"How about cereal?" Duke offered.

"Okay." Always agreeable—what wasn't to like about the boy? All he needed was a loving couple to see past his deformity and realize what a true treasure he was.

Taking a deep breath, she straightened her sweater, fluffed her hair and marched to the kitchen. "Good morning, gentlemen." She waltzed into the room, catching a flash of silver hair in her peripheral vision. She stopped at the counter and helped herself to a cup of coffee.

"Morning, Renée." Duke's quiet greeting elicited memories of their necking session on the couch the previous night. They'd snuggled in front of a roaring fire and had kissed and touched and talked as if they were in their own secluded paradise.

"Hi, Ms. Sweeney." Timmy's smile lent her courage and she joined the three males at the table.

"Dominick, this is Renée Sweeney. Renée, my stepfather, Dominick Cartwright."

One black eyebrow lifted. "The girlfriend Mr. Timmy mentioned."

"Pleasure to meet you." She smiled brightly and thrust her hand out.

Dominick's grasp was rough and callused—not what she expected of a millionaire. "A pleasure, Renée." He scowled at Duke. "You didn't mention your guest's beautiful dimples."

Ignoring the compliment—most rich people practiced false flattery—she guessed the man's age to be around sixty and assumed his olive skin, thick silver hair and shockingly dark eyebrows drew appreciative stares from females of every age.

"Morning everyone," Sam called out as she descended the stairs into the kitchen. She wore men's flannel pajamas and socks that resembled candy canes. Timmy pointed to her feet and grinned.

"Are you laughing at me?" Sam flashed a mock scowl, then bent to kiss her father's cheek before grabbing a cereal bowl from the cupboard. "Hey, Timmy, want to watch cartoons?" she asked.

"Yeah, sure."

"Bring your bowl."

Timmy scrambled from his chair and hurried as much as his twisted foot would allow. A moment later Renée heard him ask, "Can I wear your socks?"

"They're real," Sam teased. "They taste like peppermint. If you're good I'll let you eat one."

"Nuh-huh!" Timmy protested.

"The little mischief-maker claims you and my stepson are an item." Dominick stared at Renée.

Renée waited for Duke to rescue her, but the scoundrel remained stone-faced. "We're friends." Then she amended, "Good friends."

"Have you always lived in Detroit?"

"Born and raised." When Dominick opened his mouth she cut him off with a smile. "And I happen to have a real affection for the city so keep that in mind."

"I suppose the area has its merits." Dominick sipped his coffee. "And your family?"

"I was adopted as a baby."

"What about your birth family?"

"I don't have any contact with my birth parents. I entered the foster care system as a newborn. Fortunately my foster mother adopted me. She'd lost her husband, a Detroit cop killed in the line of duty, shortly before I entered the picture. At that time, her son was also a rookie on the police force."

"Your mother sounds like a special woman."

"She's been very supportive of my efforts to help the needy children in our city."

"Since Duke's mother is no longer with us, I'll ask." Then he winked at her. "What are your intentions toward Duke?"

Surprised by the question Renée stammered, "I...I—"

"Don't answer, Renée," Duke instructed. "Dominick meddles in everyone's business." He left his chair and dumped the remains of his coffee in the sink. "Ready for a tour of the ranch?" he asked her.

Dominick's contemplative stare followed Renée as

she grabbed her jacket from a hook on the wall. When she glanced over her shoulder the older man winked, then smiled, and Renée's lips curved in response.

The millionaire wasn't such a bad guy after all.

"GOT A MINUTE?" Duke hovered outside his stepfather's study, peering in at Dominick who sat at his desk, monitoring oil stocks on the computer.

"C'mon in." Dominick tossed his reading glasses on the desk and slouched in the chair. "How was the ranch tour?"

"Good. Renée's in the barn with Timmy and Matt, practicing her roping skills." Duke reclined in the leather chair across from the desk. Over the years the two men hadn't engaged in any heart-to-heart talks, but that hadn't been his stepfather's fault. Duke had resented his mother too much to give Dominick a chance.

"What's on your mind?"

Rubbing a finger over a scratch in the leather seat, Duke said, "What do you think of Renée?" He had yet to figure out why his stepfather's approval mattered.

"What's not to like about the woman? Underneath the pretty face is a crusader with a heart of gold." After a pause he asked, "How serious are things between the two of you?"

"Very." On Duke's part anyway.

"Then what's bothering you?"

"I…" Duke swallowed hard. What he was about to admit would make him sound petty and immature. "I care for Renée a lot. More than I've cared for any other woman, but I don't want to take a backseat to her job." He leaned forward. "She works harder than anyone I've met. Days, nights, even weekends." He shoved a hand through his hair. "Maybe it's immature, but I want to be her first priority, not an afterthought at the end of the day."

Dominick's leathery face wrinkled with sympathy. "When you and your mother arrived I was caught up in feeling in love again and didn't notice that Laura was trying too hard to win Matt and Samantha's affection on top of establishing herself as a Realtor in the area. In the process, you ended up being neglected."

Not only had his mother hurt Duke, but later Elizabeth had come along and had chosen her law career over a future with him. To this day none of the Cartwrights knew Duke had been ready to propose to Elizabeth the night she'd stood him up at the restaurant.

"If you and Renée are truly in love, you'll make time for each other."

"It's more than her job," Duke went on. "She harbors a grudge against wealthy people and damned if I can figure out why."

"She grew up in a different world than you did. Give her time. She'll come around." Dominick cleared his throat and changed the subject to a more comfortable one. "Have you made any business connections in Detroit?"

"Several weeks ago I received an invitation to serve on a local community development board. The group is in charge of overseeing the improvement of the Warehouse District along the Riverfront."

Dominick nodded. "Sounds like a position of influence in the community."

"The first meeting is scheduled after the holidays. We're voting on a community recreation center for the area. The board members aren't in favor of it. They've denied the applicant once before."

"A recreation center seems like a positive addition." Dominick frowned.

"I haven't viewed the plans for the project, but from the board's e-mails it sounds like the kind of facility that will cater to clientele the board would prefer to bar from the area."

"Are you going to vote no?"

"Yes, Duke. Are you going to vote against it?" Renée stood in the doorway, stunned at what she'd just overheard. Duke was a member of the community development board that Renée had been fighting against for approval of her recreation center.

A cold shiver wracked her body, leaving her numb and questioning Duke's involvement with her and the warehouse kids. All along she'd believed that Duke had genuinely cared about the kids. Now she didn't know what to think. Had he done all those nice things for them to work his way into her good graces and then attempt to ask her to withdraw her proposal? Had everything between them been a lie?

"As I told Dominick, I haven't seen the plans yet," Duke answered.

"Did you enjoy the tour of the ranch?" Dominick's question broke the tense silence between her and Duke.

Renée forced the words from her mouth. "Your ranch is beautiful."

"Good. I hope you'll visit again soon."

I doubt it. "When are we leaving?" she asked, not caring if her question sounded rude.

Duke's brow furrowed. "Tomorrow afternoon."

Not soon enough as far as Renée was concerned.

Chapter Thirteen

For the life of him, Duke didn't understand what he'd done to tick off Renée. The trip to Tulsa to meet his family had gone well until the final day when she'd overheard him and Dominick discussing Duke's upcoming meeting with the community development board. Later in the evening when he'd cornered Renée in the kitchen, he'd asked what was wrong and her sad-eyed stare had sliced through him.

"Nothing that can be fixed," she'd answered.

When he'd announced the following morning that they'd had to fly to Detroit earlier than scheduled to avoid incoming bad weather, Renée was visibly relieved the visit had been cut short.

Now they were back in Detroit on Christmas Eve day and nothing felt magical or exciting.

"Mr. D, want to play NASCAR with me?" Timmy asked from his seat on Renée's living-room floor.

"Not right now." Duke stood in the foyer waiting for Renée to get off the phone. As soon as he'd carried her luggage into the house, she'd excused herself to check in with her mother.

"Mom says hello," Renée announced when she wandered into the room, her gaze glancing off Duke's face like a boxer's blow.

He got the message loud and clear—she didn't want to discuss their relationship. Fine.

After speaking with his stepfather Duke realized his fear of competing with Renée's job for her attention was unfounded. He might have to share Renee's heart with countless children in crisis, but the idea of living without her wasn't an option. He'd fallen in love with her and he'd gladly settle for a sliver of her heart rather than nothing at all.

"Everything okay with Bernice?"

"She's baking cookies for the neighbors."

Duke feared if he didn't come up with a plan right then, he'd spend Christmas Eve alone in his hotel room. "Are you up for a round of last-minute shopping?"

"For whom?" she asked warily.

"Maybe Timmy would like to drop off a few gifts for José." It hadn't happened overnight, but Duke realized that his need to be first in Renée's life had switched positions with his need to please her. "Unless your mom has special plans for later?"

"No. She attends church service, then she and several widows gather for a Christmas Eve party."

As of this moment, Duke hadn't received an invite to the Sweeney Christmas Day get-together. "Great. Then we'd better get going. The stores close early." He called across the room. "Hey, Timmy. Make a pit stop. We're going to visit José."

"Cool!" The boy shut off the game and Duke helped him with his coat and gloves.

Ten minutes later, they parked in the lot of a big-box department store. Once inside, Timmy suggested an iPod, but Duke wasn't sure if José had access to the

Internet to download music onto the device. They agreed on a combination alarm clock-CD player and two CDs. The band members looked as if they'd been held hostage in a tattoo parlor. While Timmy added bags of candy to the cart, Renée selected practical items—socks, underwear and T-shirts. Duke tossed in a sketch pad and a box of charcoal pencils for Kenny.

As soon as the three of them entered the Covenant House the senior administrator requested a private meeting with Renée. Duke gave Timmy a tour of the facility, but José was nowhere to be found, so they waited in the recreation room. Renée emerged from the staff office, her face pale and mouth drawn into a tight line. Duke sat Timmy in front of the TV and met Renée across the room.

"José ran away," she whispered.

"What?" They'd dropped the teen off a few days ago and he'd acted comfortable with his new surroundings.

"Roger took him along for a ride in the outreach van. José recognized members of a gang from his old neighborhood. He left the van and took off running."

"And Roger didn't call you?"

"This happens a lot. They searched for him yesterday and right now Kenny and the others are out in the van driving through neighborhoods. Roger had planned to phone later tonight if they hadn't found José."

The defeat in Renée's voice scared Duke. "Let's drive over to the warehouse," he suggested.

"They already did. José's too smart to hide there." Her sigh yanked Duke's heartstrings. "All we can do is pray he remains safe until he resurfaces."

The likelihood of the teen avoiding trouble wasn't good if he joined a gang. "We left the gifts in José's room. If he shows up he'll have them."

Renée lied to Timmy, telling the boy that José had volunteered to ride in the outreach van and had already left. Outside the building, Timmy tugged Duke's coat sleeve. "Mr. D?"

"Yeah?" He lifted the lightweight into the front seat of the truck.

"There's more kids we can give presents to."

"Hold that thought." Duke stepped aside, allowing Renée to get in, then he shut the door and hopped in the driver's side. "What kids are you referring to?" Duke reversed out of the lot.

"The ones who didn't want to come to the warehouse with the rest of us."

"You should have told me sooner about these kids," Renée scolded.

Eyes wide, Timmy whispered, "We never tell on each other. That's the rule."

Dumb rule. Renée made eye contact with him over the boy's head. The earnest appeal in her gaze said she wanted to find Timmy's friends. Didn't she understand he'd do anything to make her happy? "I'm game, if you are."

She nibbled her lower lip and a bolt of heat shot through Duke. It had been too long since he'd kissed her. Touched her. Loved her.

"Most of the stores have closed. Our best bet is a supermarket," Duke said.

An hour later, they'd filled a cart with food, mittens, hats, scarves and phone cards. Renée intended to write her contact information on the cards and encourage the kids to call if they needed help. At the register Duke swallowed a silent protest when his bank account suffered another hit. Parents weren't joking when they claimed kids were expensive.

Their first stop was the Warehouse District.

"Over there!" Timmy pointed out the windshield. Several streetlights had been vandalized and the area was too dark to see beyond the vehicle's headlights. Duke switched on the high beams and slowed the truck to a crawl. "Where?" He scanned the lot filled with trash and construction debris.

Renée leaned forward in the seat. "I don't see anyone."

"That's 'cause Damian's hiding in the tunnel."

Duke faced the truck toward the lot, illuminating a cement sewage pipe. One end had been barricaded with cardboard held in place by an old tire. "How old is Damian?"

Timmy shrugged.

"Tell him who you are or he'll take off." Duke shifted the truck into Park, but left the motor running.

"Here." Renée handed Timmy a phone card. While she offered instructions on what to say to Damian, Duke grabbed one of the grocery bags from the backseat. A minute later, Timmy approached the lot and yelled, "Hey, Damian, it's me, Timmy! I got food!"

A scuffling sound met Duke's ears and the teen crawled from the pipe, but remained hidden in the shadows.

"The bag's heavy. I'd better carry it." Duke feared Timmy might stumble and fall on a shard of broken glass or discarded drug paraphernalia.

"Don't run! Mr. D won't hurt you!" Timmy shuffled forward. Duke followed at a distance. At the end of the pipe, he deposited the bag on the ground and left.

Damian stepped into the light. As Duke watched the boys knock their fists together in greeting, then engage in conversation, he struggled to get a grip on his emotions. Until he'd arrived in Detroit, he hadn't realized how much pain and sadness existed in the United

States, never mind all over the world. Kids shouldn't have to live in cement pipes or spend Christmas Eve alone and scared.

After retrieving the grocery bag, Damian accepted the phone card from Timmy. Whether the kid would sell it or use it was anybody's guess. At the truck Timmy announced, "Damian says thanks."

"Where to next?" Duke asked.

"The railroad tracks by the water tower." Timmy put on his seat belt and they drove off.

They found three girls ranging in ages from thirteen to seventeen living in a rusty boxcar. They allowed Renée and Timmy inside the car, but Duke sat in the truck, worried the girls would feel threatened by his presence. "What's their story?" he asked when the duo returned.

"Runaways," Renée answered. "The oldest promised to call in a few days. They might accept help if they—"

"Let me guess," Duke interrupted. "Stay together."

She nodded. "Kids on the run travel in packs—for protection and companionship. And they get away with petty crimes like shoplifting and purse snatching if they work in teams."

"We've got two bags of groceries left," Duke said. "Where to next?"

"Ricci said there's a boy living in the bathroom at the bus station."

"The Greyhound Station?" Renée asked. When Timmy nodded, she added, "It's on Howard Street."

A short time later Renée discovered a young boy curled behind a toilet in the women's room. Antonio was five years old and said his mother had left him to get her medicine. Duke assumed the medicine had been drugs. Antonio couldn't remember how many days his mother had been gone, but evidently she did this often to the boy. Duke worried that Antonio's mother had overdosed or become a victim of foul play. Whether Renée wished it or not, the police would have to become involved in the boy's case. While Timmy and Antonio munched on food in the backseat, Renée whipped out her cell phone and pulled off a miracle.

Mrs. Altman agreed to take Antonio for a few days. They delivered the little boy to the older woman's home along with a bag of food. Ricci and Willie were excited to see Timmy, but understandably upset that Ms. Sweeney hadn't found their buddy a home yet.

"We should call it a night," Renée suggested when they drove away.

"What about the church?" Timmy asked. "Sometimes when we get really cold we go to the church and lay on the benches."

"All right," Duke agreed. "Let's see if we can give away the last of our groceries." At almost 10:00 p.m. he parked in front of a church not far from the Riverfront. A sign on the property advertised that the doors to the worship hall would remain open throughout the night providing refuge for anyone in need of escaping the cold on Christmas Eve.

Inside they discovered a lone girl sitting near the front. Renée sent Timmy up the aisle to speak with her. The girl stood and Renée sucked in a quiet gasp. The teen was pregnant and by the size of her belly ready to give birth any day.

"When are you due, honey?" Renée asked when the teen stopped in front of them.

She cast a worried glance at Duke and shrugged.

"I'm a social worker." Renée offered her business card. "We'd be happy to take you to a hospital where a doctor can examine you and the baby."

The teen tugged her dirty sweater tighter against her body. "I don't have any money."

"The hospital won't charge you for the visit," Renée promised.

The girl didn't put up a fight, which proved she'd reached the end of her rope. When they arrived at the emergency room of the Detroit Receiving Hospital, Duke and Timmy hung out in the lobby while Renée waited with Rosemary to see a doctor.

After a short while Timmy stretched out across the small sofa and fell asleep. Duke asked the admitting nurse if she'd watch the boy while he checked on Renée and the teen, then he went in search of them.

"There are options." Duke heard Renée talking when he stopped outside the cubicle. "You don't have to give your baby away."

Duke hurt for Renée, imagining that each time she helped a pregnant teen she was reminded of her own birth mother turning her out.

"But I haven't graduated from high school. And my parents won't let me come home unless I give up the baby."

"I'll speak with your parents."

"They won't listen," Rosemary scoffed. "They kicked me out when I told them I was pregnant."

"Then I'll find a group home where you can live and receive assistance with the baby while you attend school."

"Ms. Sweeney, I don't think I'd make such a good mother."

"Sure you will."

"I don't know who the father is."

"The baby is yours, that's the important thing."

"Please, stop. I don't want my baby."

"Too bad, young lady. You can't throw your baby away because you're not ready to be a mother."

Duke had never heard Renée speak so harshly, but he suspected she was exhausted and irritable after learning that José had run away when she'd gone to great lengths to help him.

"Someone will adopt my baby and give her or him a better life."

Children having children—the situation saddened Duke.

After a long stretch of silence, Renée said, "A social worker will discuss the adoption process before you leave the hospital."

"Yeah, okay."

Renée flung the curtain aside, then froze when she spotted Duke a few feet away. Tears pooled in her eyes. "Don't say a word," she warned. "Not one word."

He followed her to the waiting room, where he lifted Timmy into his arms and carried him to the truck.

Santa's elves were calling it a night.

"IS HE ASLEEP YET?" Duke asked when Renée waltzed into the kitchen after tucking Timmy in for the night in the guest bedroom.

"The boy's pooped." And so was she—physically and emotionally. But Renée admitted if she crawled into bed right now she'd shed tears for every lost soul left out in the cold tonight. For every child she'd never be able to help. For all the pregnant teens giving birth to unwanted babies.

And most of all for herself—because the man sitting at her kitchen table had broken her heart.

"What's wrong? You haven't been the same since before we left the ranch," he said.

Renée rubbed her brow, not sure she had the strength or energy to contend with this conversation. It was Christmas Eve and she'd hoped—no dreamed—she and Duke would spend the evening making love, not breaking up. "Care for a glass of wine?" She needed a shot of courage.

"Sounds good." His stiff posture relaxed, and she felt a pang of guilt that Duke had no idea she was about to send him packing.

Don't feel bad. He was the one who played you for a fool.

She carried the wineglasses to the kitchen table and joined him. He reached for her hand and she allowed him to capture her fingers. His warm grasp sparked a flashback of making love in his hotel room. He'd fooled her with his caresses, kisses and tender words. Had she been so starved for love that she hadn't seen he'd been using her? Their entwined hands blurred before her eyes as the pain of loss—deeper than she'd ever experienced—squeezed her heart.

"You haven't said much about the visit to the ranch." Duke spoke quietly.

More sadness filled her. She'd traveled to Oklahoma with high hopes for her and Duke. She genuinely liked Duke's stepsiblings. They were nice, caring people. Even Dominick had impressed her with his kindness toward Timmy.

Duke released her hand and left his chair. He stood at the sink. "We're dancing in circles, Renée."

An image of Duke's face the morning after they'd made love came to mind. For a long while she'd watched him sleep. He'd been the only man who'd ever made her feel alive in her dark, sometimes dangerous and depressing world. She'd yearned to believe he cared deeply for her, but she hadn't been able to shake the fear that with time eventually Duke would show his true colors. She should have listened to her conscience. Instead she'd allowed Duke to sway her feelings for him. He'd snuck under her defenses and she'd believed he'd held himself to a higher standard than the wealthy people she'd dealt with in the past.

"What's happening between us?" His eyes flashed with confusion. "We're good together."

In the bedroom, yes. Outside the bedroom they were a disaster.

"C'mon, Renée. Talk to me. You can trust me."

"That's just it, Duke. I can't trust you."

His eyebrows drew together. "What are you saying?"

Trust played an integral role in a forever kind of commitment. Right or wrong, Renée refused to trust Duke. "Did you do all those nice things for the kids because you really cared or because you'd hoped to influence me to drop my petition for a recreation center?"

"What are you talking about?"

"The community development board," she answered.

"What about it?"

"I'm the petitioner of the recreation center. I'm the one the board is trying to ban from the Warehouse District." Renée ignored his wide-eyed, openmouthed gape. "Is that why you've gone to great lengths to help me with the kids—because you have a stake in the board's decision?"

Duke's face turned to stone. "You're asking me if I've been using you to advance my own business objectives?" He shoved away from the counter. When he reached her chair he pulled her to her feet. Then his mouth was on hers. Hot. Hungry. Wine flavored with desperation. Of their own accord her eyes closed. Her traitorous body didn't care if he was friend or foe. She wound her arms around his neck and pressed her breasts against his chest.

He broke off the kiss, his breathing ragged. "Did that feel like I was only interested in advancing my career?" He clasped her face between his hands. "I want seven days a week. Twelve months a year. Year after year. I want forever with you, Renée."

Eyes burning she twisted out of his hold. "Duke—"

"You would never have given yourself to me like you did if you didn't love me."

Give him that much. "You're right. I fell in love with you." She wiped away a tear. "Stupid me, I went and fell in love with another wealthy man."

"What do you mean another?"

Tell him. "I was engaged in college to the son of a wealthy family. His parents believed Sean deserved better than an adopted girl from a working-class neighborhood in Detroit."

"What happened?"

"I thought Sean loved me and would defy his parents and marry me." She swallowed hard. "But he didn't."

Duke inched closer and caressed her cheek. "I'm sorry you were hurt, but I'd never use you—"

"Even if you haven't already, you will. Our lives will always be in conflict. Your world wants to pretend my world doesn't exist. The community board doesn't want the recreation center because they believe those kinds of kids will reflect negatively on the area. They'd rather the needy be quarantined miles away and kept out of sight from the general population."

"I'll change the board's mind about the center," he vowed.

"If you hope to build a reputation of influence in the

business community you'll have to vote with the board against me."

"We'll work out a compromise."

"The rich don't compromise. In order for Dalton Industries to succeed you'll be forced to play by their rules."

"Admittedly I need my business to succeed in Detroit." He sucked in a deep breath. "I picked the one city I didn't care to live in because I wouldn't need Dominick's help. If I can stand up to my stepfather I can hold my own with a handful of local bigwigs."

"Maybe you'll succeed and change the board's mind this time. But what about the next time? Or the next?" She rubbed her brow. "Our jobs will always put us at odds. After a while our good intentions would wear thin and then we'd be miserable."

"So you're dumping me?" He held her chin between his fingers, forcing her to maintain eye contact.

She nodded, her voice buried under the wreckage of her broken heart.

He reeled as if she'd physically slapped him, then left the room. She stood in the kitchen doorway, watching him shove his arms into his jacket. He pulled a gift-wrapped box from his coat pocket.

"My father gave these to my mother on their wedding day. After he died, my mother gave them to me, confessing that she'd never loved my father as much as he'd loved her." Duke sucked in a deep breath. "I guess my father and I have a lot in common." Then he stared at Renée, his emotions in his eyes. "We both came up short in the eyes of the women we fell in love with." He tossed the box onto the dining-room table. "Merry Christmas, Renée."

The quiet squeak of the front door closing sounded like a bomb going off in the house.

The box, tied with a red bow, blurred before Renée's

eyes. With trembling hands she tore off the paper and lifted the lid. A double strand of rose-colored cultured pearls lay on a soft bed of white cotton. She clenched the pearls in her fist and closed her eyes.

Tears came hard, fast and silent.

Chapter Fourteen

The day after Christmas, Duke showed up at the police precinct where Renée's brother worked. "I'm here to see Officer Sweeney," he informed the desk sergeant.

The man buzzed Renée's brother and a moment later, the cop appeared and the two men shook hands.

"Coffee?" Rich asked.

"Sounds good." Incidental chitchat depleted, he followed the officer to a deserted break room. Rich poured coffee into two foam cups—evidently the police station hadn't gone green. "Thanks." Duke carried his brew to the table in the middle of the room.

Claiming the opposite chair, Rich muttered, "You look like hell."

"As far as Christmas's go, this one sucked." Duke had spent the day holed up in his hotel room watching holiday movie reruns and dining on room service.

"If it's any consolation, Renée's just as miserable."

The news failed to cheer Duke. He didn't wish his wretchedness on anyone—not even the woman who'd caused his.

Rich tipped the chair back. "What's going on between you guys?"

"I'm in love with your sister." He paused, waiting for

a reaction, but Rich wore his cop face—stoic, no emotion. Duke continued, "And I'm confident she loves me."

"But…?"

"She found out I'm on the community development board responsible for improving the Warehouse District along the Riverfront."

"Uh-oh."

At Rich's reaction, Duke asked, "You heard about Renée's petition for a recreation center?"

"She's worked over a year to secure the funding." Rich slurped his coffee. "Are you voting for or against the center?"

"I haven't seen the plans yet. Hell, I haven't even been to my first meeting."

"A few board members wield a lot of power in Detroit. They can make or break your business."

Exactly what Duke feared. "Whether I vote for or against the proposal, I'm screwed."

"Yep." Rich grinned.

Duke didn't appreciate the cop's sense of humor. "Although I pledged to convince the board to approve Renée's project she's adamant our careers will always be in conflict."

"She's had a few run-ins with wealthy people during her lifetime that haven't worked out in her favor."

"After learning what her fiancé's parents did to Renée in college and her situation with the development board I sympathize with her grudge against the rich. But wealth aside, I've got a gut feeling that Renée doesn't believe she's entitled to the same happiness as others. And I don't understand why."

Rich stared into space, blinking rapidly until the sheen of moisture disappeared from his eyes. "You might be right, Dalton."

The ticking clock sounded like a drum banging in the room. After a tense thirty seconds, the cop left the table and tossed his half-empty coffee cup into the trash can. "C'mon. There's something you need to see."

Another maze of hallways led to an office the size of a school classroom, crowded with police desks. Rich's station sat next to a window. He motioned to a grouping of framed newspaper articles hanging on the wall.

"Baby Found in Dumpster Saved by Rookie Cop"

"Detroit Dumpster Baby Survives"

"Dumpster Baby Attends First Day of Kindergarten"

"Dumpster Baby Enrolled in College"

"Famous Dumpster Baby Graduates with Honors"

"Detroit's Famous Dumpster Baby City's Newest Social Worker"

Dear God. Renée had been thrown out with the garbage. Duke's chest constricted until he worried his lungs might burst. With each wheezing breath he concentrated on maintaining his composure.

"After all these years it still gets to me," Rich confessed, then cleared his throat.

Rage unlike anything Duke had ever experienced pulsed through his bloodstream, lighting his veins on fire. Fury and pain rendered him speechless. He collapsed into the chair next to the desk, rested his hands on his thighs and braced himself.

"It was Christmas Day—rather night. My partner and I were patrolling the west side around Brightmoor. We were searching for gang activity when we drove past an alley and spotted a couple of teenagers hanging around a Dumpster. The teens took off before I got halfway down the alley." Rich glanced at the wall. "Then I heard a noise."

A rude snort escaped the cop. "Swore it was a

damned cat meowing." He shifted in the chair as if the memory agitated him. "I opened the Dumpster lid and flashed my light. And there she was—stuffed inside a white trash bag lying on top of the garbage heap."

Shit. Duke swiped angrily at the tear that escaped his eye.

"Luckily, the plastic had ripped and she'd been able to get enough oxygen to stay alive. I tore open the bag and almost lost my supper. She was covered in afterbirth and so damned blue, like one of those Smurf cartoon characters." Rich paused, lost in the memory.

"I wrapped her in my jacket and ran to the patrol car. On the way to the hospital, she'd stopped breathing but I gave her CPR and she hung in there. My partner had called ahead so the doctors and nurses were waiting when we pulled up to the E.R.

"She was a fighter." Rich smiled. "As soon as her body temperature rose and the doctors got fluids in her, Renée cried like a banshee." The smile faded. "My mom chose the name Renée. It's French for *reborn*. Renée had been left for dead, but she'd come back to life right there in my arms."

"Renée said Bernice was her foster mother first." The words exited Duke's throat in a choked whisper.

"Yeah. My father had been murdered a few weeks before Renée came into the picture. I think Mom needed Renée more than Renée needed her."

Duke glanced at his lap, surprised to find his fingernails imbedded in his thighs. With concentrated effort he forced his hands to relax. "I'm afraid to ask how Renée being left in a Dumpster relates to wealthy people."

"Ever heard of the Caleone family?"

"I haven't been in Detroit long enough to learn who the movers and shakers are," Duke admitted.

"The Caleones made their fortune in the automobile industry. They go way back to the Henry Ford era. Over the years various family members have entered local and state politics."

"Anyway—" Rich cleared his throat "—I volunteered to work Renée's case, but the police chief handed everything over to his top investigator who closed the case within a week, leaving Renée just another abandoned-child statistic."

"What about the delinquents loitering around the Dumpster?"

"They came up clean. Then one day out of the blue a couple of girls from a private high school in Bloomfield phoned the precinct. I happened to be on duty and took the call. The girls were worried about a friend who'd been missing from school since September—the Caleones' daughter."

"Isn't Bloomfield north of Detroit? Why would they contact this precinct?"

"When the Caleone girl stopped attending school her friends called the family, but no one would speak to them. The same went for the faculty and administrators at the school they attended. The girls then contacted their local police and were told it was a family issue and to mind their own business. That's when the teens recalled that their friend had been dating a guy from Brightmoor. So they called here for help."

"Were you able to locate the boyfriend?"

"Nope. My partner and I paid a visit to the Caleones, but all they'd say was that their daughter flew out east to live with relatives and attend school."

"A week later a woman identifying herself as the Caleone housekeeper got in touch with me. She said the Caleones daughter had given birth in the home on

Christmas Day, but that the baby had been taken away."

"Unbelievable."

"We figured the Caleones paid a scumbag high on methamphetamine to dispose of the baby."

Duke's head pounded, but he refrained from interrupting, wanting—no, needing—to hear the entire story.

"We confronted the Caleones with the new information, but got nowhere. Not long after, the housekeeper vanished with no forwarding address."

The story was straight out of Hollywood.

"Our luck dried up. The Caleones wielded their mighty influence and suddenly the police chief threatened to fire us. My partner gave in. But I was young and cocky and kept digging around in the case. Then the boss hinted that my mother might not be able to adopt Renée." Rich shrugged. "I buried the shovel and never asked another question."

"Hey, Rich." An officer poked his head around the doorway. "Meeting in ten."

"Whatever happened to your boss?" Duke asked.

"The chief retired a few years later. Moved to Florida."

"Is Renée aware she might be related to the Caleone family?"

"When Renée turned eighteen I told her what I knew about her case. At the time she didn't seem to care. Then years later the missing Caleone *daughter,* Patricia, wife of Senator Nielsen of New Hampshire, showed up in Detroit with her husband for a political fund-raiser. Her picture was in the newspaper—she was the spitting image of Renée. Renée had just graduated from college when she'd seen the photo."

"What did she do?"

"She showed up on the Caleones' doorstep and asked

to see her mother. When Patricia walked into the room, Renée introduced herself as the infamous Detroit Dumpster baby."

Duke closed his eyes and imagined the scene that had unfolded that day in the Caleone mansion. Had Renée been angry and frightened or hopeful her mother would claim her?

"Renée wouldn't talk about the confrontation with anyone afterward, except to say that her mother had acted as if she had no idea who Renée was before instructing the butler to show Renée out."

This time when Duke stared at his hands he envisioned his fingers wrapped around a regal white neck.

"You're right about my sister believing she isn't entitled to her own happiness," Rich conceded. "Her mother's rejection probably affected Renée more than any of us ever guessed."

"No wonder she doesn't trust the wealthy."

Rich nodded. "She resents that the privileged are allowed to live by a different set of rules and standards than the rest of society."

"I'm not like the Caleones," Duke protested. "I don't lie, steal, cheat or break the law to achieve my goals."

"Maybe so. But wealth naturally breeds power and influence. That makes you the enemy in Renée's eyes."

"How do I prove to Renée that I'd never use who I am or the money I earn to put myself ahead of the less fortunate?"

"Figure out a way to show my sister that good can come from power and wealth, too." Rich stood. "Whatever you decide…" His voice trailed off and he shook his head. "She's been hurt enough for one lifetime."

As soon as Rich left the room, Duke approached the window and stared at the street below, cursing the knot in his throat. After all he'd done for Renée and the kids… After making love to her… Damn it! She should *know* he was different. Better than those who'd betrayed her in her past.

Out of the corner of his eye he caught a movement—a kid hovering in the doorway of a building. Loitering? Or trying to escape the bitter cold? Where would he sleep tonight?

Duke would never again be able to see another street urchin and not think of Renée. He had to find a way to make her believe she was entitled to the same love and happiness she worked tirelessly to secure for the kids in her care. And Duke had to succeed in convincing her that he was the man who could give her that happy ever after.

By chance, the kid glanced up at the precinct building, his gaze connecting with Duke's. Suddenly Duke knew what he had to do—regardless of the cost to his pride or his business reputation in Detroit.

LORD, SHE MISSED DUKE.

Renée had been in a blue funk since Christmas Eve when she'd broken up with Duke. Each time she recalled the despair on his face when he'd tossed the pearls onto her dining-room table—as if his heart had been inside the gift-wrapped box—she wanted to weep.

Without Duke's help, the warehouse children, save José, would never have slept in a warm bed Christmas Eve and awoken to gifts under the tree. Renée had asked her brother to search for José, but the teen had yet to surface on the streets.

Then there was Timmy. Always the one left behind. Left out. Just plain left. If Renée had the means she'd adopt the little boy, but he deserved a real family—

mother, father and siblings. As for the girls in the box-car—when she'd checked on them, they'd vanished.

Antonio, the little boy left at the bus station, had been taken from Mrs. Altman's care and placed in a temporary foster home. His mother's body had been discovered in an alley near the bus station—an overdose of crack cocaine.

Damian, the teen who'd camped out in the cement sewage pipe by the Riverfront, had disappeared, also. Too many children swallowed up by the city.

A glance at her calendar confirmed Renée's appointment tomorrow at 10:00 a.m. with the local community development board. What would she say to Duke? She eyed the jewelry box peeking out from her tote bag under the desk. She'd brought the pearls to work for the past two weeks, intending to slip them into a mailing envelope and return them to Duke. Each day she'd chickened out.

She'd convinced herself that she and Duke had nothing in common—an easy and convenient excuse to end the relationship. But the cold hard truth was that Renée loved Duke. Whether he wore a three-piece suit or a city sanitation uniform, Duke would always be the kind-hearted, generous man she'd lost her heart to.

Not a day went by that Renée didn't ask *why me?* Why hadn't her birth mother wanted her? She assumed she possessed a defect obvious to others, but unknown to her.

Yet when she attempted to picture herself living a different life her mind went blank. If not for having been thrown away in a Dumpster, Rich wouldn't have found her. She wouldn't have been raised by Bernice, who taught her the value of every human life—regardless of ethnicity, wealth or upbringing. She would never have become a social worker and helped the hundreds of children she'd taken under her wing over the years.

Why was it so difficult to let go of her past? Didn't

she deserve happiness as much as the children she served each day?

Renée set the jewelry box on her desk and lifted the lid. She studied the pearls blurring before her eyes— perfect pink effervescent balls. Then she flipped open the small piece of paper with Duke's message.

Renée: please accept these pearls as a token of my love. They represent the beauty and hope you bring to so many needy children.
Yours always, Duke.

Renée doubted she'd ever cease being wary of the wealthy—after all, she was only human. But the time had finally arrived to stop paying penance for who she was and where she'd come from. To let go of the anger and resentment she'd held tight all these years. To allow herself to trust in Duke's love for her.

"Renée." Harriet stood in her office doorway.

"Yes?"

"The police department phoned. There's been a report of kids living in a warehouse along the Riverfront."

Forcing her face to remain neutral, she asked, "Which one?"

"The Screw & Bolt Warehouse."

Oh, no. Hadn't Duke demolished that building yet? Good grief, he must be furious.

"Get out there and remove the kids before the media finds out." The office door shut in Renée's face.

A thousand thoughts crowded her mind as she put on her coat. And the pearls.

The drive to Atwater Street took less than ten minutes. She parked the wagon in front of the warehouse and stared through the windshield at the chaos. No crane with a wrecking ball, but plenty of construction vehicles and men in yellow hard hats swarmed the parking lot.

There! Duke's trademark Stetson stood out in the crowd. Heart pounding she soaked up the sight of him.

Standing near the hood of his truck, he studied a large sheet of paper—blueprints? Duke spoke to the man at his side, then they both laughed. Renée's heart melted. Lord how she'd missed the cowboy and his sexy grin.

She crossed the lot, forcing herself to take measured steps when she yearned to sprint. She hovered a few feet away from Duke, content for the moment to feast her eyes on him. Then the other man noticed her and stopped talking. Duke turned. Their eyes met. And clung. *You look good, Duke.*

God, you're beautiful.

I'm sorry.

Me, too.

"I've missed you, Renée." His quiet confession caused her eyes to sting.

"I've missed you, too."

Duke noticed the pearls and his eyes widened. "You're wearing the necklace."

"Yes, I am."

"Does that mean…?"

"It does."

His callused hands cupped her face. "I love you, Renée. You're generous and caring and you've got a heart as big as Detroit beating inside that beautiful body of yours." He kissed the tip of her cold nose. "All I want is a tiny piece of you to call my own. That I don't have to share with anybody. The entire city and every child in it can have the rest of your heart."

"Oh, Duke," she whispered, tears escaping her eyes and dripping over his fingers.

"I want to share my life with you. The good and bad of both our worlds. I want to be there for you at the end of the day—to hold you, kiss you. Love you." He leaned forward and whispered, "Turn around."

Puzzled, she gaped at the huge red ribbon strung across the front of the warehouse.

"You're viewing Detroit's future children's shelter."

"I don't understand," she whispered.

"A safe haven for homeless kids to live and attend school until foster homes become available. And the plans include a recreation center."

Renée's throat closed off and she struggled to breathe. "But what about the community development board?" she choked.

"We met yesterday. I proposed a new plan that combined your recreation center with a children's shelter and the entire project would be housed within my company's building. Once the board realized all the positive press they'd receive they jumped on the bandwagon."

Duke hugged her tight. "And you're in charge of the whole program. I've already spoken with your boss. Harriet agreed that you'd be the perfect candidate to run the shelter."

Renée laughed. "Only because I'll be out of her hair." Afraid to believe the miracle she asked, "What about Dalton Industries?"

"The offices will occupy the upper two floors of the building. The other three will house dormitories, a kitchen, classrooms, and the bottom floor will be the recreation center."

"How can you afford this, Duke? The money I raised for the center won't make a dent in the cost."

"I can't afford it, Renée." His face sobered. "But my stepfather can. The shelter is a gift from Dominick. What do you think of the name Santa's Shelter?"

"I love it," she whispered, her throat tight with emotion. Renée knew what it had cost Duke to seek his stepfather's help. He'd put aside his pride for her and all the needy children in the area.

"Marry me, Renée. Make me the happiest man in the world."

She wrapped her arms around his neck and went up on tiptoe, pouring her heart into the kiss.

"Is that a yes?" he asked.

"That's an *I love you. This* is a yes." She kissed him again and again and again. Then Duke swung her around in a circle. "I hope you're ready to become a mother right away."

Right away? Her face heated, then spiked in temperature when Duke's husky laugh echoed through the air. His gaze softened as he stared into her eyes. "Yes, I want to have babies with you, Renée, but I was thinking we'd need practice first."

"Practice?"

"With a nine-year-old."

What was he saying?

"I want to adopt Timmy. If I have anything to say about it, that boy is not spending another Christmas without a family of his own."

Heart bursting with joy, Renée basked in the miracle Duke had pulled off. A month ago she'd never have believed that the once crumbling, desolate Screw & Bolt Factory Warehouse would represent hope, love and a brighter future for all of Detroit's needy children.

* * * * *

Detroit Daily Bulletin
February 2009—"Dumpster Baby Weds Son of
Oklahoma Millionaire"
September 2009—"Santa's Shelter Opens Its Doors"
December 2009—"Thanks to Santa, City's Homeless
Children on the Decline"

*Be on the lookout for Marin Thomas's next book
featuring Matt Cartwright—and the woman who
finally lassos the stubborn cowboy!
Available in April 2009,
only from Harlequin American Romance.*

Here is a sneak preview of
A STONE CREEK CHRISTMAS,
the latest in Linda Lael Miller's acclaimed
McKETTRICK *series.*

A lonely horse brought vet Olivia O'Ballivan to
Tanner Quinn's farm, but it's the rancher's love that
might cause her to stay.
A STONE CREEK CHRISTMAS
Available December 2008
from Silhouette Special Edition

Tanner heard the rig roll in around sunset. Smiling, he wandered to the window. Watched as Olivia O'Ballivan climbed out of her Suburban, flung one defiant glance toward the house and started for the barn, the golden retriever trotting along behind her.

Taking his coat and hat down from the peg next to the back door, he put them on and went outside. He was used to being alone, even liked it, but keeping company with Doc O'Ballivan, bristly though she sometimes was, would provide a welcome diversion.

He gave her time to reach the horse Butterpie's stall, then walked into the barn.

The golden retriever came to greet him, all wagging tail and melting brown eyes, and he bent to stroke her soft, sturdy back. "Hey, there, dog," he said.

Sure enough, Olivia was in the stall, brushing Butterpie down and talking to her in a soft, soothing voice that touched something private inside Tanner and made him want to turn on one heel and beat it back to the house.

He'd be damned if he'd do it, though.

This was *his* ranch, *his* barn. Well-intentioned as she was, *Olivia* was the trespasser here, not him.

"She's still very upset," Olivia told him, without turning to look at him or slowing down with the brush.

Shiloh, always an easy horse to get along with, stood contentedly in his own stall, munching away on the feed Tanner had given him earlier. Butterpie, he noted, hadn't touched her supper as far as he could tell.

"Do you know anything at all about horses, Mr. Quinn?" Olivia asked.

He leaned against the stall door, the way he had the day before, and grinned. He'd practically been raised on horseback; he and Tessa had grown up on their grandmother's farm in the Texas hill country, after their folks divorced and went their separate ways, both of them too busy to bother with a couple of kids. "A few things," he said. "And I mean to call you Olivia, so you might as well return the favor and address me by my first name."

He watched as she took that in, dealt with it, decided on an approach. He'd have to wait and see what that turned out to be, but he didn't mind. It was a pleasure just watching Olivia O'Ballivan grooming a horse.

"All right, *Tanner*," she said. "This barn is a disgrace. When are you going to have the roof fixed? If it snows again, the hay will get wet and probably mold…"

He chuckled, shifted a little. He'd have a crew out there the following Monday morning to replace the roof and shore up the walls—he'd made the arrangements over a week before—but he felt no particular compunction to explain that. He was enjoying her ire too much; it made her color rise and her hair fly when she turned her head, and the faster breathing made her perfect breasts go up and down in an enticing rhythm. "What makes you so sure I'm a greenhorn?" he asked mildly, still leaning on the gate.

At last she looked straight at him, but she didn't

move from Butterpie's side. "Your hat, your boots—that fancy red truck you drive. I'll bet it's customized."

Tanner grinned. Adjusted his hat. "Are you telling me real cowboys don't drive red trucks?"

"There are lots of trucks around here," she said. "Some of them are red, and some of them are new. And *all* of them are splattered with mud or manure or both."

"Maybe I ought to put in a car wash, then," he teased. "Sounds like there's a market for one. Might be a good investment."

She softened, though not significantly, and spared him a cautious half smile, full of questions she probably wouldn't ask. "There's a good car wash in Indian Rock," she informed him. "People go there. It's only forty miles."

"Oh," he said with just a hint of mockery. "*Only* forty miles. Well, then. Guess I'd better dirty up my truck if I want to be taken seriously in these here parts. Scuff up my boots a bit, too, and maybe stomp on my hat a couple of times."

Her cheeks went a fetching shade of pink. "You are twisting what I said," she told him, brushing Butterpie again, her touch gentle but sure. "I meant…"

Tanner envied that little horse. Wished he had a furry hide, so he'd need brushing, too.

"You *meant* that I'm not a real cowboy," he said. "And you could be right. I've spent a lot of time on construction sites over the last few years, or in meetings where a hat and boots wouldn't be appropriate. Instead of digging out my old gear, once I decided to take this job, I just bought new."

"I bet you don't even *have* any old gear," she challenged, but she was smiling, albeit cautiously, as though she might withdraw into a disapproving frown at any second.

He took off his hat, extended it to her. "Here," he teased. "Rub that around in the muck until it suits you."

She laughed, and the sound—well, it caused a powerful and wholly unexpected shift inside him. Scared the hell out of him and, paradoxically, made him yearn to hear it again.

* * * * *

*Discover how this rugged rancher's
wanderlust is tamed
in time for a merry Christmas, in
A STONE CREEK CHRISTMAS.
In stores December 2008.*

Silhouette®

SPECIAL EDITION™

FROM *NEW YORK TIMES* BESTSELLING AUTHOR

LINDA LAEL MILLER

A STONE CREEK CHRISTMAS

Veterinarian Olivia O'Ballivan finds the animals
in Stone Creek playing Cupid between her and
Tanner Quinn. Even Tanner's daughter, Sophie,
is eager to play matchmaker. With everyone
conspiring against them and the holiday season
fast approaching, Tanner and Olivia may just get
everything they want for Christmas after all!

*Available December 2008
wherever books are sold.*

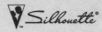

SPECIAL EDITION™

MISTLETOE AND MIRACLES

by *USA TODAY* bestselling author
MARIE FERRARELLA

Child psychologist Trent Marlowe couldn't believe his eyes when Laurel Greer, the woman he'd loved and lost, came to him for help. Now a widow, with a troubled boy who wouldn't speak, Laurel needed a miracle from Trent...and a brief detour under the mistletoe wouldn't hurt, either.

Available in December wherever books are sold.

HARLEQUIN® *Romance*®

Marry-Me Christmas

by *USA TODAY* bestselling author

SHIRLEY JUMP

A *Bride* FOR ALL *Seasons*

Ruthless and successful journalist Flynn never mixes
business with pleasure. But when he's sent to write a
scathing review of Samantha's bakery, her beauty and
innocence catches him off guard. Has this small-town
girl unlocked the city slicker's heart?

Available December 2008.

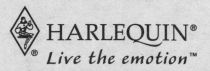

HARLEQUIN®
Live the emotion™

REQUEST YOUR FREE BOOKS!
2 FREE NOVELS PLUS 2
FREE GIFTS!

Love, Home & Happiness!

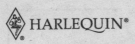

HARLEQUIN®

American ★ Romance®

COMING NEXT MONTH

#1237 A BABY IN THE BUNKHOUSE by Cathy Gillen Thacker
Made in Texas
When Rafferty Evans offers the very pregnant Jacey Lambert shelter from a powerful rainstorm, the Texas rancher doesn't expect to deliver her baby! Now, with five cowpokes ooh-ing and ahh-ing over the new mom's infant, can Jacey help the handsome widower open his heart to the love—and instant family—she's offering?

#1238 ONCE UPON A CHRISTMAS by Holly Jacobs
American Dads
Is Daniel McLean the father of Michelle Hamilton's nephew? As Daniel spends time with the young Brandon, and helps Michelle organize Erie Elementary's big Christmas Fair, the three of them come to realize a paternity test won't make them a family. But the love Michelle and Daniel discover just might…

#1239 A TEXAN RETURNS by Victoria Chancellor
Brody's Crossing
Wyatt McCall just blew back into town, still gorgeous, still pulling outrageous stunts like the ones he did in high school. And the stunt he's planning this time around could reunite him with the woman he loves. Mayor Toni Casale, who still hasn't gotten over Wyatt, has no idea what the Texas bad boy has in store for Brody's Crossing—and for *her*—this Christmas!

#1240 THE PREGNANCY SURPRISE by Kara Lennox
Second Sons
Sara Kauffman is lively, spontaneous, playful—everything Reece Remington is not. Although he's only visiting the coastal Texas town where she lives, Reece has a surprisingly good time helping Sara run a local B&B. Could this buttoned-down guy be ready for an entirely different kind of surprise?

www.eHarlequin.com

HARCNMBPA1108